Praise for *The Proper Words for Sin*:

"I've been a fan of Gary Fincke's for ma. ___ ___ ___ ___ collection just confirms what I already knew—namely, that Fincke ___ story writer of uncommon gifts. These new tales are subtle yet powerful, passionate but clear-eyed. Fincke lets his characters breathe while making the reader hold his or her breath. This is what I want from fiction. It's *all* I want from fiction."

—Steve Yarbrough, author of *The Oxygen Man* and *Safe from the Neighbors*

"'You can learn to live with anything,' one of Gary Fincke's characters thinks in a moment of wonder, denial and sorrow. The stories in *The Proper Words for Sin* feature heroes whose justifiable fears and intractable losses become necessary lessons in the strangeness and fragility of life. Sometimes mordant, occasionally bitter, Fincke's people counter their everyday terrors not with any flighty hope but sheer gritty determination. Welcome to Pennsylvania. Fine, close work from a master."

—Stewart O'Nan, author of *Snow Angels*, *The Odds*, and *Emily, Alone*

"Richly detailed and generous. A moving collection."

—William J. Cobb, author of *The Bird Saviors*

"Powerful, insightful, and cut to the bone."

—Joan Connor, author of *How to Stop Loving Someone*

Praise for other work by Gary Fincke:

"Gary Fincke writes wonderfully quirky, unpredictable stories full of vivid characters and unforgettable details and moments. There's a lovely, hilariously wry sense of humor at work here, but there's also a truly heartfelt compassion for the lives of ordinary working folks—those little failures and triumphs that make a reader gasp in both recognition and wonder."

—Dan Chaon, author of *Among the Missing* and *You Remind Me of Me*

Gary Fincke is the Writers Institute Director and Charles Degenstein Professor of English and Creative Writing at Susquehanna University. Winner of the 2003 Flannery O'Connor Award for Short Fiction, the 2003 Ohio State University/*The Journal* Poetry Prize, and the 2010 Stephen F. Austin Poetry Prize for recent collections, he has published twenty-four books of poetry, short fiction, and nonfiction, most recently *The History of Permanence* (poems); a memoir, *The Canals of Mars*; *The Fire Landscape* (poems); *Sorry I Worried You* (stories); and *Amp'd: A Father's Backstage Pass*, a nonfiction account of his son's life as a rock guitarist in the band Breaking Benjamin. His work has appeared in such periodicals as *Harper's*, *Newsday*, *The Paris Review*, *The Kenyon Review*, *The Georgia Review*, *Ploughshares*, *American Scholar*, and *Doubletake*, and has been read by Garrison Keillor on NPR. He has twice been awarded Pushcart Prizes for his work, including "The Canals of Mars," which was reprinted in *The Pushcart Essays*, an anthology of the best nonfiction published during the first twenty-five years of the Pushcart Prize volumes.

He has been recognized by *Best American Stories* and the O. Henry Prize series, and cited eleven times in the past thirteen years for a "Notable Essay" in *Best American Essays*.

Gary Fincke grew up near Pittsburgh and currently lives in central Pennsylvania.

THE PROPER WORDS FOR SIN

Vandalia Press, Morgantown 26506

Copyright 2013 by West Virginia University Press

All rights reserved

First edition published 2013 by West Virginia University Press

Printed in the United States of America

21 20 19 18 17 16 15 14 13   1 2 3 4 5 6 7 8 9

PB   1-935978-88-8 / 978-1-935978-88-6

EPUB   1-935978-89-6 / 978-1-935978-89-3

PDF   1-935978-90-X / 978-1-935978-90-9

Library of Congress Cataloging-in-Publication Data

Fincke, Gary.

[Short stories. Selections]

The proper words for sin / Gary Fincke. -- First edition.

p.   cm

ISBN 978-1-935978-88-6 (Paperback : alk. paper) -- ISBN 1-935978-88-8 (Paperback
: alk. paper) -- ISBN 978-1-935978-89-3 (ePub) (print) -- ISBN 1-935978-89-6 (ePub)
(print) -- ISBN 978-1-935978-90-9 (pdf) (print) -- ISBN 1-935978-90-X (pdf) (print)

1. Short stories, American. I. Title.

PS3556.I457P76 2013

813'.54--dc23

2012041398

The individual chapters of this book have been previously published as follows:
"There's Worse," *Witness* (O Henry Citation) 2005; "The Out-of-Sorts," *CrazyHorse*
2008; "The Fierceness of Need," *CrazyHorse* 2007; "Weepers," *South Carolina Review*
2010; "All the Big Things," *South Carolina Review* 2013; "Private Things," *Beloit Fiction
Journal* 2009; "The Proper Words for Sin," *Black Warrior Review* 2005; "The Promises
of Labels," *Texas Review* 2006; "Somebody Somewhere Else," *Cimarron Review* 2010
"You Can Look This Up," *Cimarron Review* 2008; "The Blazer Sestina," *Willow Springs*
(George Garrett Prize) 2003.

Cover design by David Drummond. Art direction and page design by Than Saffel.

THE PROPER WORDS FOR SIN

STORIES BY

GARY FINCKE

VANDALIA PRESS

MORGANTOWN 2013

For Derek, Shannon, Aaron, and, as always, for Liz

CONTENTS

THERE'S WORSE

"I WAS RIGHT THERE," my mother said every time she told the story, "that close to being nuked. It's one of God's mysterious ways that your mother is here to talk about it."

By the time I was seven, I had that story memorized, how there really was a nuclear bomb, but only the TNT in the trigger device went off when it hit the ground after accidentally falling from a B-47 just taken off to Germany. What's more, my mother had clipped every news item she'd ever found about the incident, and once a year, on its anniversary, March 11th, she'd get out the scrapbook and sit for an hour reading on the couch.

After a while she'd pat the cushion next to her and invite me to sit down to listen. "Your mother was just a girl," she'd tell me at the beginning, so it sounded like *once upon a time,* and I loved that story all the way up to when I was twelve, the same age she'd been on that day in 1958. The crater the bomb had made was thirty-five feet deep, she'd explain, and then my mother would look from the picture of the hole in the ground to me in a way that said, *Doesn't this just pass all understanding?* "What do you think, Eddie?" she'd finally say. "That family, the Greggs, should have been dead when the bomb hit their house, and yet they all lived. And me less than a half mile away in my Dad's car—what do you think should have happened to your mother?"

That story about the atomic bomb falling on South Carolina always kept my mother talking as if the warning it held was meant only for our family. I knew that, even when I was young. The rest of the world could hear her talk about the books she read and the movies she'd seen, none of which meant anything to our future, but the accidental atom bomb was just for us.

Even so, my father never sat down on the couch or in a chair in the living room while she was talking. He was already sick of hearing that story, even when I was in second grade, saying, "Not that again, Deenah," from the kitchen or the bedroom while she talked.

"Can you imagine us if the real bomb had gone off?" she would say then, putting her arm around my shoulders.

"No," I'd say at once, because I was pretty sure she would have disintegrated, and I couldn't imagine my mother as a cloud of dust.

"Give it a goddamned rest, Deenah," my father would shout. He never came closer than the open doorway to the dining room.

My mother would pause when he swore. She'd shift her eyes to the stairs and say, "The girls, Willy," even though they were asleep or, beginning the year I turned ten, watching television like they always did before bedtime.

I had two sisters, Iris and Rose. Both of them were what polite people called mentally challenged, but at school, in the halls, I could hear kids saying "retard" sometimes when Rose and I happened to pass each other. Rose, the older, was in sixth grade and in the same building.

She went to regular classes in the morning and the "special room" in the afternoon, a program that made sure she stayed in the right grade, passed along each year to keep her with the other students her age. Iris was in third grade, at least for two hours a day. Hardly anybody even knew I had another sister. Either way, nobody joked about my family like they did other kids'. Joey Palozzi, for instance, who had eight brothers and sisters, was "the good Catholic." Jamie Czak, whose mother was fifty-five, was "the accident." Rose was only eleven months younger than me, and I wished, some days, that my friends called me "son of the horny."

The day I turned twelve, my mother took me aside as if she'd heard plans for that nickname. "After Rose was born, we were going to stop. We'd decided to have two children, and Willy wanted them bang, bang, just like that, to put a start and a stop to that sort of goings on." She hesitated right there like she wanted to make the rest of the story "Chapter Two," and I kept my eyes on the cake shaped like a football she'd just lifted from the oven, giving her time to go on or to go check on my sisters.

"But after a while," she finally said, "when anybody could tell Rose had her problems, your father wanted another. To make up for Rose. To replace her. I let him have his way. I thought it was for the best."

They were both teachers. They worked in the same building because they'd gotten their jobs years ago before the school had changed its policy, making it a rule a husband and wife couldn't both work there, because it looked too much like unfair hiring.

"And what's the chance of a husband and wife both being good?" my mother had said once, meaning, I thought, for me to understand my father wasn't good at what he did.

We lived in the neighboring school district because my mother didn't want me or my sisters to attend her school. "Not because I wouldn't want to have you in class," she'd said, "but you should know the school where I teach isn't very good, and it would be worse for your sisters."

My father had grimaced, and she'd stared at him. "Isn't it?" she'd said. "Isn't it awful?"

"My God, Deenah," he'd said.

"Go ahead, then," she'd said. "I want to hear this. Go ahead and tell him what's good about it."

My father didn't answer, but I knew what she meant. The school was out in the country, and hardly any of its students went on to college. It wasn't about behavior; it was about ambition. To make things worse, my father taught business math, all of the courses taken by students who would never read another book after they turned in their senior exams.

My mother taught English, and saw every student for two straight years in 11th and 12th grade. By the end of their first month with her, she knew how few cared to read, but she gave me junior and senior English lessons every night: "Catharsis," she said. "That's a good one. Denouement. Epiphany."

* * *

My father, until I turned ten, talked in a code I couldn't crack. "There's more of the same," he would say. My mother would nod as if she knew exactly how much and what kind.

"I know what you're thinking," my father would say, and she would do an odd shuffle up the stairs, Rose and Iris each holding a hand of hers with their other arm wrapped around her legs so that they needed to side-step, nearly backwards, in order to climb without falling.

"God's handiwork," my father would call. Even when I was in third grade, like Iris is now, I thought I understood what that meant.

I didn't solve those expressions. They just disappeared, replaced by words that were vague but somehow clear: "The girls need their mother," and "Let the good times roll." Some nights, after my sisters were in their room, my mother would ask him if he enjoyed being mean, and every time he answered, "Does it sound like it?"

When they argued, my parents would stand facing each other, always in the kitchen, the only room they seemed to share, and my mother would finally stop talking and say, "A hug, Willy. It's time for a hug."

Whenever I was around, she would use the same exact words, cadenced with a caesura as if she were breaking the line from a poem during one of my evening high school English lessons. Each time my father would hesitate, not looking at her, and then give in, embracing her, making sure, I thought, that he held on long enough that she wouldn't ask again, not that night, at least. "That wasn't so hard, was it?" she'd say, and then we'd all smile, the memories of small cruelties taking a few steps back, silent in the shadows like guards.

Only once did I overhear them "make up" when I wasn't in the room. "A hug, Willy. It's time for a hug," my mother said. I'd been watching television downstairs, shutting it off in the moment my mother spoke. I sat there, picturing my father hesitating, my mother standing still like she always did.

A moment later, when I didn't hear her say, "That wasn't so bad, was it?" I tensed, leaning toward the stairs as if that could help me know what they were doing. "What are you so afraid of?" I heard her say, and then, shortly thereafter, "You're sick. You know that?" and I knew my father hadn't moved.

I held my breath. I didn't hear footsteps, or even the creak of the floor above me that would signal either one had changed positions. When, a minute later, someone moved, I sucked in air and knew it was my mother because the footsteps walked to the stairs and came directly down. She paused at the bottom and looked at me. "You satisfied?" she said. She took the remote from my hand, turned on the television, and sat in the other chair, finding a movie and staring at the screen in a way that made me get out of my chair and go upstairs, where my father had opened a beer and laid open the skinny magazine that came with the Sunday paper, just beginning to pencil in letters above the Cryptoquote, putting in the As and the Is, his pencil hesitating above the word with an apostrophe, trying to decide whether it was a contraction or showed possession. He held the pencil in the same place until I left the room.

* * *

"March 11, 1958, Florence, South Carolina," my mother was saying. "Walter Gregg was the father in that house that was hit by an atomic bomb."

She had the scrapbook open on her lap. It was New Year's night, four months after my twelfth birthday, and she had Rose on the couch beside her. I watched from the doorway while she turned two pages, and then I sat in a chair, facing her like a student. "Anytime it could happen, Rose," she said. "Boom! Just like that, right beside our car."

"No, it won't," I said. "That's impossible."

My mother turned another page as if I hadn't spoken, but Rose made a motion with her arm as if she were throwing something at me, and my mother looked up. "That's what the army said back then," she said.

"Well, it is."

"You keep saying that when you're going up in smoke."

I wasn't going to admit I'd thought about that a hundred times. A thousand, probably. I sat there watching Rose beginning to squirm, my mother going on as if she didn't need an answer from me. "Every day of my life," my mother said, "I've thought about how my brother and my parents and I could have gone *poof* just like that. It would have taken a while for somebody to figure out what had happened to us. We'd have been a regular mystery for a while and then some."

"Maybe forever," I said, and she smiled.

"Yes," she said. "That's what I think sometimes. So far from home like that, nobody would ever have known what became of the Warrens."

Rose's hair fell to her waist, and my mother, using both hands, held it out like wings. "Just look at this," she said.

I waited for Rose to slap my mother's hands away, but she stared straight ahead as if there were a mirror in front of her, a way to watch how others saw her long brown hair. Just then my mother let the hair fall back down and began to stroke it near the scalp as if she were combing it.

Rose lifted her chin, and her eyes seemed to fix on the ceiling. "Like a dog," I thought and wished I hadn't. My mother's fingertips made shorter and shorter strokes until she seemed to be feeling for something on my sister's skull, as if the reasons Rose would never "grow up" could be detected by touch.

I tried to imagine Iris sitting beside my mother, listening to the atom bomb story. She had hair so short, strangers took her for a boy, and she talked nonstop, pausing only when my mother gave her a signal by pressing a fingertip to her lips. "OK, Mommy," Iris would say, and for a minute, sometimes two or three, she would press her lips so tight they'd turn white.

Sometimes she'd forget to breathe, and her eyes would open wide, as if she were surprised. It was worse, those times, than having her chattering, "We're having cherry pie for dessert. See it sitting there where Mommy put it? It's for dessert. It's cherry pie. I like cherry pie. It's my favorite. We're having it for dessert. After we eat our vegetables."

At dinner, when her lips burst apart in a puff of air, there'd be little bits of food that would shoot onto her plate and the table. By then my father would be watching television, waiting for my mother to send me downstairs to call him back for dessert.

"What's five divided by ten?" my father would ask Rose as he ate his pie, and when she'd shake her head and say nothing, he'd look at Iris, who'd say, "Five-and-ten-cent store," rapping her fork on the table, spouting, "Murphy's. Woolworth's. Montgomery Ward's."

* * *

For as long as I could remember, my father said all that was important was that my sisters were happy, and that they were learning to take care of themselves. It sounded like something a teacher would say, and I'd stopped believing him two years before, as if turning ten allowed me to notice the way his face tightened when he talked about my sisters.

When we were out, my sisters clung to my mother. Rose, taller and heavier than I was, bumped against her as they walked, sometimes jostling her off-balance. Iris, tall and skinny, gripped my mother's hand, swinging it as they walked. At first people would smile, thinking how nice it was, and then they'd show recognition and turn away, their eyes pitying or relieved, especially if they had children of their own.

"There's worse," my mother would say, "way worse." As if someone else's misfortune made our lives better.

A week after Rose had been taught the bomb story, my mother started talking as soon as dinner began. "You know what I just found out?" she said.

Nobody answered, not even Iris, so I said, "What, Mom?"

"Something went wrong in a nuclear reactor in Oklahoma today. Somebody got killed and who knows how many were hurt."

My father sighed and started to cut his roast beef. "You know what it is?" my mother said. "It's the twenty-third nuclear accident since 1952. It's only a matter of time."

"That's enough, Deenah," my father said.

"Think about it," my mother said, "One of these days it will be so bad we won't be reading about it in the newspaper."

"Why not?" Rose said. My mother, surprised Rose had spoken, looked at my father as if she hoped he had an answer.

"Well," she finally said, "it's just that if there's big news everybody always watches it on television."

"Like the Super Bowl?"

"Yes. Just like that."

"Bears and Patriots," Iris said. "Number XX."

That night my mother walked into my room five minutes after I'd turned off the lights. "You never know," my mother said, "what can happen." I blinked and squinted and waited for her to keep going, to tell me a story or name something, but she just stood by my dresser, picking up and putting down each of the Star Wars action figures I hadn't touched in a year. She looked at Chewbacca the longest, as if she were trying to make out his face under all that hair.

After she left, I found an empty shoebox and scooped all of the action figures into it. I pushed it into a back corner of my closet with my foot.

* * *

The next day we drove to Harrisburg. "To shop for bargains," my mother said, but on the way home, my mother, like she always did, pointed out Three Mile Island. "They think they know everything," she said, "and just look at that."

I knew she wanted everyone to pay attention to the cooling towers that didn't have steam issuing from their tops, the ones that rose above the shutdown reactor. In the backseat, like I did on every trip, I sat between Rose and Iris, because otherwise, as my mother put it, they would "get after one another." "We're only two miles away right now," she said, "if that thing went boom!"

"Mommy," Rose said. "Are we going to hell?"

My mother stared at my father. "Who told you that?" she said without turning toward the backseat.

I saw my father's eyes look into the rear view mirror, and Rose put her head down as if she were going to pray. "Good one," my mother said, and Iris started to clap, keeping it up until I grabbed her wrists and held them, listening to her scream and hearing my mother say, "Perfect," just before my father pulled off the road and stopped, Iris shutting up just like that, as if her voice quit when the car wasn't in motion.

"If you're so stuck on 1958, why don't you tell him about your first period?" he said, and the car got so quiet I could hear a series of tiny thumps from something small loose in the trunk.

My father turned on the radio then, a rock station our mother let us play when she drove, and though he hated rock and roll, he left that station on as he pulled back onto the highway, John Mellencamp singing about how he was going to live and die in a small town. I remember that song the way I remember trying to guess what was rolling loose in the trunk, deciding it was a golf ball. "You ought to be ashamed," my mother said, but only when the car was parked in the driveway.

My father turned around and looked at Rose. "Three oranges are fifty cents," he said, "a dozen oranges is?"

Rose looked at her shoes. Iris, sitting up straight, tapped the back of the seat near his head and shouted, "A box of doughnuts."

My father grinned. "Chocolate," Iris went on. "Jelly-filled, cream-filled. Glazed."

Before he got out of the car, my father snapped off the radio, and I remembered him telling me once that the battery would run down if I left the radio on when the car wasn't running, and I'd thought he was trying to teach me something, until my mother, driving one day a week later, didn't touch the radio when she got home, and he reached over to turn it off. "For God's sake, Willy," she said, "you think that makes a difference?"

* * *

My mother began to turn on the news at exactly six o'clock each night. If an atom bomb had gone off somewhere, it would be the lead story, she said. There was no sense tuning in ten minutes late when the stories would be about triple murders and oil spills.

Pretty soon, though, nearly every night began with the upcoming launch of the Challenger, because Christa McAuliffe, the teacher, was on board. My mother made sure we ate dinner by 5:30, and she abandoned the dishes of leftovers on the table until she'd checked the news. My father and I picked at whatever she left out for dessert while Rose and Iris dug into pies or cakes or ice cream. "Blueberry," Iris shouted triumphantly, spraying crust and filling the night before the shuttle was finally, after days of delays, scheduled to go up, "cherry, apple, strawberry, peach!"

"Are we safe?" my father said each night, passing her on the stairs to watch ESPN. "Can the dishes be washed?"

I thought that my parents had settled for staying together even though they weren't close, that they'd learned how little they loved each other and lived with that. But after that day in the car I could see they had more they could lose, and it was gone. When my father came upstairs at seven o'clock, I started studying in my room or just listening to my small clock radio, leaving the television to Rose and Iris. I could hear my parents' voices, and even without words, I knew they were arguing, my father finally slamming a door to end it, though I couldn't tell whether my mother still said, "A hug, Willy. It's time for a hug."

* * *

A cold wave settled down from Canada, one that reached all the way to Florida where the shuttle was poised for takeoff. Our science teacher gave us Xeroxed completion questions about the history of the space program with stencils of the Challenger on either side. *Launch Yourself to Knowledge* had been printed across the top of every worksheet, even the ones about the cycles of water, since the middle of January.

Of course, when it looked as if the teacher were taking off at last, all of my section, 7A, hoped she'd go up while we were in class so we wouldn't have to do anything but watch television for forty-five minutes, but it was so cold in Florida, the flight was postponed for another day.

"They act like it's a big deal, but that shuttle is safer than Florida's citrus crops," my father said at dinner that night.

"Then what are all those smart men waiting for?" my mother said.

My father crossed his knife and fork in front of him as if he were forming a food-related coat of arms, but he looked puzzled, laying the knife across the fork in a T before he said, "For the fruit to freeze."

"Exactly," my mother said, and my father jabbed the knife blade between the points of his fork, pretending to saw.

"Five grapefruit for a dollar," he said to Rose. "Four oranges for sixty cents," and Iris sat up straight. My mother laid one hand on

Rose's head, ran her fingers through her hair, and stood. It was only quarter to six, but she disappeared downstairs, taking her half-filled plate with her.

"What do you think, Eddie?" my father said. "Will they ever send a whole family up together in the space shuttle?"

"I don't know," I said, but it sounded more unlikely than another accidental atomic bomb.

Later, even with my radio turned on, I could hear my parents arguing, but their voices were loud for less than a minute before I heard Iris's shrill laugh and my mother dragging my sisters up the stairs, the three of them clomping along like losers in a sack race.

"Look at this," my father said that evening when I came downstairs at ten o'clock for a glass of milk. He was filling in the final letters of the Cryptoquote. It said, "MacArthur, the sailor, declared, 'Old fishermen never die, they just smell that way.'"

"You should try these," he said. "They keep you on your toes."

The letters all looked clean and sharp, as if my father had discovered the solution by fathoming patterns and frequencies and whatever else you needed to finish these things. He dropped his pencil into a small mug on the kitchen sideboard and walked away. Usually he left the solved quotes on the table, the paper folded into a quarter of a page, the puzzle face up, but this time, he'd handed it to me, and when I examined it, I could see he'd erased nearly all of the stray marks from his early guesses, a stray E above where he'd printed O, and what looked to be an S at the end of the word that ended in D.

* * *

"I'm sorry," our science teacher said the next day when our class ended at 11:20 and the countdown hadn't reached fifteen minutes. "It looks like the 7Bs get to watch the lift off."

So we were at lunch when the shuttle lifted off at 11:38 and didn't know it had blown up until we walked into history class at 11:50. There wasn't a television in that room, so all we could do was talk and imagine, thinking about the teacher who was dead.

That afternoon, when my father and mother got home, all five of us watched the shuttle lift off and explode twice. Rose climbed onto my mother's lap, and I held Iris while my father stood behind our two chairs through the second rerun. "Look at that," my mother said. "Just imagine." My father walked upstairs before she switched to another station where they were showing the launch again.

Twice more we watched, and each time, no matter what I'd seen before, I thought it might make it, that it would keep on going until it disappeared like all of the other shuttles that were so boring we'd stopped watching them on the school televisions. My mother leaned forward every time we heard, "Roger. Throttle up," and the flame shot down the shuttle's side just before the explosion. Rose began to cry, and Iris watched her instead of the television as my mother found a fifth rerun.

"It's a bomb, that thing," she said. "They put people inside a bomb and hope they're lucky."

I wanted to ask if she thought the teacher was in tiny pieces, but I kept my mouth shut. Finally, after the shuttle had blown up again, my mother didn't change the channel, and somebody on the television guessed that all of the astronauts had blown up instantly. Immediately, another person said that it was possible they'd lived, some of them at least, and were conscious after the blast, not dying until they'd fallen back to earth.

"Listen to that, Eddie," my mother said. "Just when you think you know the worst." She shut the television off and ordered two pizzas to be delivered. "Pepperoni," she said into the phone, "extra cheese," the girls both clapping when they heard those words.

For the first time that year, no one left the table early. We stuffed ourselves, finishing every slice, and nobody asked about dessert or made for the television. "Denouement," I wanted to say, "epiphany," imagining how well I would do someday on a high school English test.

My father pushed his chair away from the table. "Well," he said, "that takes care of that."

"What?" my mother said. Her hands were in her lap, but I could see them curl into fists.

"The pizza, Deenah," my father said. "Jesus Christ."

Iris picked up her three crusts and slapped them against her plate. "Jesus, Mary, Joseph, God, Christ!" she shouted.

* * *

Hours later I couldn't sleep, so I was awake at 12:44 when I heard someone moving in the hall. *Mom*, I thought, hearing her make a small noise as she breathed. Not quite a moan or a wheeze, it was something like a whimper, like a baby falling asleep after a bout of crying. For a minute, as I listened, I thought she was sick, that she had been walking late at night like this for weeks without me hearing her, and I was frightened, thinking she was keeping her illness from me, that she might be dying. I heard her pause at my sisters' door, and then I knew she was gradually opening it, because the night-light began to illuminate the hall.

I listened to my mother make that baby's voice three times, and then she nudged my door open so slowly I thought for a moment that the person in the hall wasn't my mother at all, that I'd been mistaken and there was a thief in our house, something I couldn't imagine—a woman come to steal.

I lay there without moving, one arm tucked so tightly under me I felt it going numb. She stopped making that sound, and I thought if I moved she would know I was awake and be angry at me for hearing her. It will only be a few seconds, I thought, and then she'll go back to bed, but a minute went by, the clock turning to 12:47, and she didn't move.

It was just after the number changed that I thought she was deciding whether or not to kill me, that she wanted my father to wake up in the morning and find me not breathing. It was impossible, of course, but already I was regretting that my right arm, the one I used for everything, was asleep, thick and useless if she meant to overpower me.

It seemed like a long time that I lay there thinking like that, but when she was finally gone, shuffling back to her room, the noise she'd been making returning, I took two breaths before the clock jumped to 12:48.

In the morning, after she'd cut up a grapefruit and placed a bowl full of its sections in front of me, she looked like my mother always looked. How foolish, I thought. I was as stupid as my sisters to be afraid of my mother. She'd just been checking up on me, making sure everything was all right, that nothing about me had changed.

In six weeks she'd be sitting on the couch with her scrapbook, and I knew, even if Iris joined Rose beside her, what I wanted to ask. How did the Greggs act after the bomb fell on their house? Did they love each other more? Did they appreciate what they had?

THE OUT-OF-SORTS

THE STORY WASN'T ON ANY of Stu Werner's assigned pages. He copyread sports, but he paid attention to every line of the article about the woman who'd kept the police at bay with three poisonous snakes because that woman was his mother. Though they weren't described, Stu could picture each of those snakes, distinguishing one from the other by the colors and patterns his mother had pointed out half a dozen times when he visited and she guided him to the large glass tank in her living room to look at the copperheads.

According to the article, the police had kept their distance. His mother had swung them, all three in one hand, as she gave the officers an earful. The standoff, the police reported, had lasted nearly an hour, a long time to handle poisonous snakes. And time enough, apparently, for a cluster of cops to show up from all over the county. "Once the call on the radio said she was swinging snakes, pretty much every cop from anywhere nearby showed up," the police chief said. Stu could imagine the whole lot of them, each one more useless than the next. If she hadn't been bitten on the arm and the face, they might still be standing there, a policeman admitted, "But once we saw her in distress, we used the Taser on her to get things under control."

There wasn't a word about how the police handled the snakes, but there was a paragraph about his mother's state of mind, how she'd seemed incoherently angry, the kind of attitude the police associated with drugs or alcohol. "The woman appeared to be intoxicated," the article said, "but our first job was to make sure she didn't die from those bites."

And all of that because someone had reported excessive noise—the Walczyks, her neighbors in the double house where she lived, the ones who said, "We were just fed up with her rock music coming through the wall like thunder."

The newspaper office where Stu was sitting while he read was a large loft apartment furnished by nineteen desks and twenty-one chairs, the extra two creating a makeshift waiting room beside the secretary to the editor's desk, a place where family members with obituaries sat for a few minutes before submitting their home-made eulogies. Where people fidgeted while clutching wedding announcements or self-written articles about the achievements of their children. Some people were determined to bring their news personally, and though everything they carried, most of it semiliterate, would be rewritten or discarded, their earnestness prevented him from joining in the jokes that the rewrite woman made by reading a few sentences she introduced by saying, "Listen to these howlers: 'He was the proud founder and owner of an erection business. He was a distributor of a variety of condiments.'"

Near the end of the room farthest from the editor's office was the desk Stu shared with two sports stringers who filed stories only on weekends—high school football and basketball mostly, unless there were championship games in soccer or field hockey, sports that drew the interest only of parents and friends of the players. During the summer, he'd discovered, he had the desk to himself.

His supervisor, Ralph Herrold, was two desks away, his

workspace surrounded on three sides by head-high partitions that he decorated with photographs of his two dogs, terriers that wore bandanas or sweaters in every picture. "I was here before computers made everything so easy," he'd declared early on, and Stu called him "The Master" to his girlfriend whenever he had one, the name followed by verbs like "sucks" and "blows."

He'd had three girlfriends in the eleven months he'd worked at the newspaper, but there had been several months between each one, enough that Stu had spent more time without a girl as with one. The third one had been gone for a month now. There was no telling, he thought, when he'd find another.

Down near the end of the article, in the paragraphs continued on page eight, was the information that the snakes were being held at the police station. "They scared me to death," the police secretary was quoted. "Nobody told me, and here they were when I came into the office this morning."

"We're stuck with them," the chief said. "They're evidence, for now." There would be follow-ups, for sure. His mother had been charged with reckless endangerment and disorderly conduct. Stu wondered whether resisting arrest would be tacked on, but the reporter, Jack Ferrence, didn't mention it. Ferrence would love having this story, one that could last a few days, one that everybody would follow, curious just how crazy someone might be to use copperheads as a hand-held weapon. Whether something like this would go to trial. Whether the snakes would be taken to court so a jury could see the weapon in question.

And sure enough, the case was already morning-show material on the radio, the deejay and his female sidekick laughing at 7:15, when they used the morning paper as a source for jokes. "The funniest story since Santa Claus got shot with a BB gun in the Christmas parade," the woman said.

Nowhere in the article was there a mention of his mother's medical condition. She'd lapsed into a coma for twelve hours before awakening. From the antivenom the doctors had given her, not the bites themselves. Like everything that happened late at night, it had taken a full day for the news to reach the morning paper.

* * *

There was silence about his mother at work that afternoon, not the usual joking about the erratic behavior of people who made the paper, the reporters telling stories over coffees and Cokes. Stu knew that if nobody had recognized the name, they would have mentioned the three fingers of Medusa before the day was over.

When he asked Ralph Herrold for an extra half hour at dinnertime, Herrold didn't demand a reason. He stroked his mustache with his thumb while he tapped three fingers of his other hand on his desk, creating a tiny drum roll. Stu looked at the terriers, unable to tell them apart because their scarves were the same color and pattern. A few seconds went by until Herrold said, "Well, Werner, we'll see you at 7:45 then."

"People come by more than they should," his mother said as soon as Stu walked into her hospital room. She looked at the ceiling and sighed before she added, "I know why."

She stared at the ceiling for so long, Stu glanced up as well. Nothing was there, not even a maze of cracks. "They're professionals, Mom," he said.

"That doesn't mean they don't want to take a look at the snake woman." At last, she looked at him. "You're the only person I know who's showed up. I half expected Jesse to come by worried about his snakes."

A long shot for that scenario, Stu thought. His mother had never talked about where Jesse was from or how they'd met. For years men had followed his mother home from the bar where she served tables. Not the worst men, she would say, coming into that place. "Imagine if I worked at the Top Dog or Knuckles, the sort that come in there. Wife beaters, that's who goes in there. And worse. I just get the lonely and the out-of-sorts."

Stu pictured the empty glass tank. Those snakes had always seemed to keep their distance from each other, coiled in different corners or under the flat, angled stone or the chunk of gnarled driftwood. It was a large cage, as big as a coffee table. For more than half a year the tank had sat across four chairs moved from the dining room. "I haven't sat on those chairs for years," his mother had said. "It won't hurt to get some use of them." The chairs faced each other in pairs like they had in the dining room, but the arrangement still looked unstable to Stu, who was sure that all of the clothes Jesse had hung in his mother's closet would have fit inside that tank. Jesse had told her he'd be back for the snakes, but it had been two months and there was no sign of him.

"Here," Stu said. "Maybe this will brighten the day." He'd brought a card he'd picked out after searching three shops before work. "Just hanging on?" it said on the cover, a python with a sad face dangling from a tree limb.

"There's nothing like a good meal to cheer you up," it said inside, the smiling python wrapped around a man in one of those hats that city slickers always wear in jungle movies. *A pith helmet,* Stu suddenly remembered. Even the name sounded like a fool would wear it.

His mother smiled.

"I couldn't find a copperhead card," he said.

"You should write one then," she said. "I bet it would be as cute as this one." She handed the card to him as if it had grown heavy. "I get my own room because the police want to keep an eye on me," she said. "If one of theirs had been bitten, I'd be in the penthouse."

Or dead, he left unsaid. The room was bare of decoration. If his mother left, dragging the bedclothes out the door with her, it would be ready for the next patient immediately. He propped the card on the empty nightstand, the sad-faced snake peering toward the door.

* * *

The next morning, Stu was still in bed when the radio deejays mentioned the follow-up story. "It's like a *Snakes on a Plane* sequel," the deejay said. "*Snakes in a Living Room*." His sidekick laughed as if she'd heard something hilarious.

At work the night before, Stu had avoided examining the local section of the paper because Herrold or Ferrence or one of the others would have known what he was looking for. But now, Stu retrieved the paper from his doorstep and opened Local, finding that the article filled three-fourths of a column on page three. "Snakes to Appear before District Judge," was the title, but except for the first sentence and the last sentence—a hearing was scheduled; the snakes would be presented as evidence—every word was lifted from the first published story—the snakes, his mother's name, the details of the stand-off. Jack Ferrence might have spent fifteen minutes on the article, pasting in paragraphs until he filled enough column inches to allow for a real estate ad beneath it.

Stu didn't mention the article when he returned to the hospital. If the hearing was scheduled, the police knew his mother was out of danger, that she was going to be released.

She had the newspaper lying on the nightstand beside his card.

"That reporter, he's never once said anything about who I am or what I look like or what I have to say. Not once."

"That's true."

"What kind of reporting is that? People think I'm stupid or crazy or a major lush. They imagine me all bedraggled like a bag lady. You should write the story, start it way back when your father left." She paused as if she were considering going further back, even before his father had left, when Stu was in high school, before he told Stu, one morning at breakfast, "I need to go before I get too old to have a second chance."

"And of course Jesse would be in it," she went on, "and how I came to know those snakes and how much of a pain in the ass the Walczyks are for complaining, us in a double so they're right there on the other side of the wall. Inches away and yet they call the police. It's a wonder they don't need ten more cops in just this town with so much lack of communication."

Like she had the day before, his mother looked at the ceiling, but Stu kept his eyes on her face. "You read those articles and wonder what happened to the snakes after they used that stun gun on me? You and I both know those cops would have run for it if I'd dropped them after they zapped me."

"Probably."

"That's because I put those snakes away before they fired. They didn't use that stun gun because they were afraid for me with the bites and all. They used it when I put down my weapon."

"They emptied the tank though."

"You can bet your ass they didn't get near those snakes. They brought in somebody with the know-how, a pet store owner or somebody like that, to gather up the copperheads. That reporter never says a word about it and expects everybody to think the police took care of everything."

"You can say that when you go to court, Mom. How you surrendered."

She touched the bandage on her cheek and then the one on her arm. "They were there to take me to the nut house," she said. "That's what would have happened, right? They looked me up and saw who I was and came to take me away. I recognized one of them who drove me there last year when I had that dark spell before Jesse came along. I didn't want to go back. I wasn't hurting anybody but myself. Those pricks next door should have just told me to settle down."

"They said they asked you once before a week ago."

"That's what makes them pricks. They think asking once makes them good neighbors."

His mother was right, Stu thought. The police kept records of everything, including women who'd been hospitalized for depression, if they'd had to drive them there. "You were afraid. You thought they would hurt you."

"Those snakes just panicked is all," she said. "If the cops had just stayed put instead of always inching closer, I would have been fine."

She touched the bandages again, this time in a way that made Stu think she might tear them off and throw them. Her gestures were so repetitive he felt heavy, as if he wouldn't be able to stand if he sat in the chair beside her bed. "You relax for a few minutes, Mom. I'll be right back."

Stu rode the elevator to the ground floor and walked into the cafeteria to get coffee. His shift at the paper started in an hour, and he hated the coffee that perpetually brewed there.

At three o'clock, the cafeteria was nearly empty, just two women sitting with cans of soda, their backs to each other four tables apart. Heat lamps shone above covered trays that held hours-old, unseen food. Stu poured his coffee quickly and sipped it as he rode back up to his mother's room.

He sat the heavy paper cup on the nightstand and picked up the newspaper. "Let me show you something," he said.

He turned to page five, covering his mother's story, and laid the paper out on the bed. "Watch this," he said, taking a pen from his pocket, and he began to mark the errors.

Extra capital letters on *enchilada* and *tortilla,* as if the names of international food were proper nouns. Titles not italicized, spaces missing or too wide between words, margins uneven. His mother looked pleased. She squinted at the margins and the gaps between sentences and words. "I showed May Walczyk the paper once. I told her to read a page from the local section and a page from sports and tell me which one had the most problems. She didn't see anything wrong. 'It's the newspaper,' she said. 'Why would they make mistakes?'"

Stu folded the paper and replaced it on the nightstand. He tugged the get-well card wider so someone might see the happy python inside. When he dropped his paper cup into the wastebasket, the mouthful he hadn't finished splashed against the side of the can.

"Somebody came by while you were gone," his mother said. She seemed happy to have kept that news from him for fifteen minutes. "I'm not going to jail, sweetheart. And not the loony bin either."

"Good."

"At least not yet. I have a hearing in a week, but the lawyer they sent over said I'll likely be 'looked after' when all this is said and done. They have a name for it, the lawyers, but I'm to be babysat no matter what they call it."

"He was in and out of here fast."

"She. No more than a girl. Is that how you get your start being a lawyer, taking care of people like me who don't have money?"

"In her case, at least," Stu said. "Anyway, you'll be in your own house, that's what's important. Everybody but her or whoever they send will be trespassing."

"Will they now? They'll think I'm fine and dandy in a month or two?"

"A little longer, maybe."

"It'll be like going to college. I'll have to go to class for years, and then they'll give me a send-off like I learned something to be proud of."

"College wasn't bad. Classes were the easy part."

She darkened. "People think that you got kicked out for being stupid," she said. "It breaks my heart."

"It was my call."

"Yes, it was. You and your hard head. I didn't know whether to be upset or proud."

Stu's roommate had snapped the arms off the chairs in the lounge on each floor of the seven-story dorm. Methodically, from highest to lowest. "Cheap shit," he'd said. "If these were any good, I couldn't do it."

Stu had followed him, sitting on couches while Brad Moser flexed his arms as if the chairs were exercise equipment. It was 4 a.m., and not one person was awake on a Tuesday. When Moser was finished with the chairs on the first floor, they walked outside, and Moser smoked a cigarette while Stu looked at the sky. "This place is so full of people who are sure they know something," Moser said. "I don't think they know shit."

Moser tossed his butt down and fobbed himself back inside, but Stu stayed outside. Breaking the chairs had been asinine, but Stu had been so fascinated he was still excited. Ten minutes later, he remembered he didn't have his key fob. Security, making its rounds, identified him as being awake and just outside the damaged dorm at 4:30 a.m. "The student was uncooperative about his reasons for being outside," the report said. "When the extensive damage was ascertained, he became a suspect."

"I couldn't break the chairs like that," Stu had said. "I'm not strong enough. That's all I have to say."

"I saw another student with the suspect when I passed the dorm earlier," the report went on. "Only one room light was on in the entire dorm, and the location was ascertained to be the suspect's room."

When they'd questioned Moser, he didn't deny anything. He just said, "Prove it." His biceps were huge. He was wearing a sleeveless t-shirt.

Stu had been suspended. "No matter what we can prove, we know you were an accessory," the Dean had told him. "At the very least, you didn't do anything to stop it."

"I didn't break anything," Stu had said. "If I'm a witness to a crime, I don't get arrested for refusing to testify."

"You should want to help security officers. They make sure this place is like home."

"Whose home?" he'd said, and taken the fall. A month later, Moser quit school after failing three courses.

It didn't matter that Stu had been suspended from college before he finished two years and didn't return. He'd gotten fifty-nine out of sixty on the editing test at the *Daily News*, the highest score ever. Fifty-six was the previous best, he was told. And passing was fifty, as if catching five errors out of six was acceptable. He'd missed *February 29, 2005*, and he was still angry about it because *29* was more like a trick than a problem. It wouldn't come up. Nobody would make that mistake, not in a year that didn't have the extra day.

Ralph Herrold had told Stu that somebody had spotted the *29* in the past, but that person missed six other mistakes, even making an error out of something correct. "He works here still. Ask him about it," Ralph Herrold had said, pointing to Chuck Yarnell, who proofread the local section so poorly that Stu had stopped talking to him after a week.

* * *

Jack Ferrence's next article, half a column long, had only one new sentence—the date of the preliminary hearing. To be sure, Stu laid the earlier article beside the newspaper and matched the lines. Identical. Every other word was pasted in.

That night, as Stu was eating a barbecue sandwich by himself just before seven o'clock, Ralph Herrold sat his coffee cup on the table. "Eating alone is bad for your health," he said.

Stu regretted going into one of the two restaurants that were only a block from the newspaper office. He usually walked another three blocks, sometimes more, to places where his co-workers weren't likely to go in the forty-five minutes they had for dinner. "Not as bad as hot dogs and French fries with company," Stu said, remembering the meal he'd seen in front of Herrold as he'd walked past him and two reporters before taking a booth as far from Herrold's table as possible.

Herrold didn't smile. He wrapped both hands around his mug in a way that reminded Stu of how he'd been told to sit in first grade while the teacher read a story to the class. "You unhappy at the *Daily News*?" he said.

"Sometimes." The word didn't seem to surprise Herrold, who nodded once without losing eye contact.

"*Sometimes* can seem like *frequently* to others," Herrold said. "Or even *always*, you get my drift?"

"Clear as this water," Stu said. He held up his half-filled glass in what he thought was a comradely way, but Herrold's gaze stayed fixed on his face. The water rose and fell in tiny waves until Stu laid the glass down on the table. "The *sometimes* are when I see how many mistakes get by other copyreaders. I want every section of the paper to be perfect."

"It's not healthy wanting everything to be perfect," Herrold said. "If everybody was like that, where would we be?"

"In a better place."

"You sound like a funeral director. You give it some thought and you'll see that it's just the opposite."

* * *

The last time Stu had spent an evening with his mother before Jesse left, Jesse had taken the snakes from the tank and held them in one hand while he drank beer from a can he held in the other. "Just like in them churches," he'd said, laughing, those copperheads writhing in a way that made Stu get up from his chair so he was better prepared to move. Jesse held them until he finished the beer. His mother looked happy to be standing beside a man holding three snakes within striking distance. Her expression didn't change when Jesse laid the snakes back in the tank. "To think," she said.

"Those snake handlers in church get bit some times," Stu had said. "People die."

"Really?" his mother said and bent down to peer through the glass as if she'd never thought about it.

The snakes were slithering into places that seemed sheltered— two in corners and one under the overhang of the stone. Jesse smiled at Stu in a way that made Stu think he wished Stu hadn't mentioned those snakebites. "Could one of those kill me with its fangs?" his mother said.

"No," Jesse said. "Not likely."

"Not likely." Stu's mother repeated the phrase as though she were committing it to memory. The snakes settled. Within seconds, they looked bored. Stu thought they welcomed Jesse lifting them out because it was the only time they ever acted like snakes, their bodies rippling, their eyes alert, tongues flicking.

"You ever consider just letting them run loose?" his mother said. She'd been drinking beer with Jesse since Stu had arrived two hours before, and Stu had begun to worry that a six pack mixed with her antidepressants was a bad idea, or worse, that she'd stopped taking the medicine, expecting the beer to brighten her mood.

"In the house?"

"Yes. That's who they are. Isn't that right? Things that would find their own homes."

"That's crazy. There's nothing to eat in a house like this."

"But that's not why you won't let them loose."

"It doesn't matter why not. We're done talking about this."

His mother tapped the glass, but the snakes didn't react. They acted like nothing mattered except to be picked up and carried.

* * *

After the snakes were put down, Ferrence finally interviewed somebody again. "We took them to court," the police chief said. "Their part in this was over."

"Thank God for that," the secretary said. "Two weeks of those things coiled up in that glass box sitting on the floor like that. I thought they'd get out for sure."

They were about three feet long, the article said, and when the diction began to sound like somebody besides Jack Ferrence's, Stu googled "copperheads" and discovered that Jack Ferrence had gone online to the first site available. "Copperheads are venomous pit vipers. Copperheads account for more cases of venomous snake bite than any other species. Fortunately, their venom is the least toxic of our species. Bites from copperheads are very seldom fatal; however, a bite may still produce serious consequences."

Ferrence hadn't bothered to change the syntax. "Copperheads will not usually bite. However, the bite will be readily used as a last defence."

He'd even spelled *defense* like the British, as if the copperheads had been imported from London.

Stu saw, before he clicked off, that there was an ad on the first page of the site: "Having a picture of the copperhead on a mug or coaster is a great way to keep a reference image available to use for the next snake you encounter." Stu had never seen even one snake except in the zoo or in the pet store or in his mother's living room. He imagined himself being better off to have a photograph of Ralph Herrold on his mug. One in which he was holding his sweater-clad dogs.

Once Ferrence went back to writing his own words, there were errors. *It's* instead of *its*. The plural of *lawyers* with an apostrophe as if their position earned them an extra punctuation mark. The kinds of errors fourth graders thinking about video games might make. Chuck Yarnell hadn't corrected them.

The next-to-last paragraph finally quoted his mother: "I'm sorry this happened. I don't want people to be afraid of snakes."

"She didn't look as crazy as people following this story might think," the article ended, "but there's no doubt this is the wackiest story of the year so far."

* * *

At least his mother was living at home again, sentenced to a year's probation and mandatory alcohol rehab, when the news of the snakes' death reached her. "They could have given those snakes to a zoo or some such place as that," she said. The bite on her face, Stu noticed, was nearly healed. It looked as if there wouldn't be any scar at all.

"They do the same to dogs that bite is how they figure it, Mom."

"Those snakes had names," she said. "Hal and Ed. After my brothers, God rest. A car crash and the man's cancer, who would have seen that coming? The accident could have happened to anybody, but the cancer, at thirty-four? Ed just didn't believe he could have a problem like that so young."

"I think that kind is for the young, Mom," he said.

"That's leukemia. That's for boys and girls both."

"There's more."

"Then it's a wonder any of us are left standing."

Stu nodded. All the evidence pointed that way. "I got to know those snakes," his mother said. "They were easy to tell apart. And they acted different. You know. That third one I called Jesse. He thought it was cute, but he didn't know my brothers are dead. And him just thirty-six and maybe seeing me looking older every day."

Stu stayed quiet, waiting to see which direction his mother's talk was going. She hadn't had a drink since her run-in with the police, and she seemed wound up. "Jesse, he'd pick them up and say, 'Don't this beat anything you've ever seen?' You remember him saying it was just like those people in those churches you hear about, how those snake handlers think they're closer to God with poison right there in their hands."

"Yeah," Stu said. "I heard that, for sure."

"He made me hold one," she said. "He said it was a test of my feelings for him. 'You just wait,' he said. 'You'll be different after.' He was half right about that. I was the same person, but I saw him differently. That's one test of love. I know what he saw in me was going dim, and he thought maybe this would brighten it."

After he left his mother's house, Stu looked up snake handlers. Seventy-three people had died handling snakes in church the year before. Right below that statistic was the Bible verse those snake handlers cited: "In my name shall they cast out devils; they shall speak with new tongues; They shall take up serpents; and if they drink any deadly thing, it shall not hurt them." Mark 16:17-18.

Stu knew that snake handlers were not supposed to drink alcohol. He knew they thought doctors were unnecessary. His mother handled snakes because she knew how, not because she believed in anything.

* * *

The next day, he visited again, and his mother showed him an incorrect headline and an incorrect picture caption in the Sunday paper, the edition Stu never worked on. "I'm starting to see these," she said. "Pretty soon I'll be picking at those bitty things you see. Why, this boy in the picture must wonder how he got into the wrong uniform."

"He won't see it, Mom."

"Why not? There it is plain as day, and he lives right here at the college where the paper must come every day."

"Those kids don't read the local paper, believe me. They don't give two hoots about what happens here."

She brightened. "So they wouldn't know I was the snake woman?"

"No. They never heard of her."

"They're not missing much, but it's nice to know I could walk around that place, and nobody would be the wiser."

"They don't think they live there," he said. "They think they're on vacation."

"People don't know what it's like having the police force their way in on you."

"It got out of hand, all right. It was overreaction."

"They like it, those men," she said, and glanced at the empty glass tank in a way that made him believe she missed those snakes like people miss dogs they've had put down. "You think that's true?" she went on. "That the police like to force themselves on people."

"Sure," he said. "Some part of anything is always awful."

She went to the tank, and when she reached inside, he held his breath because there was a chance she was going to dig at the dirt and pebbles as if she expected to find eggs, or would fling handfuls of the stuff around the room.

A moment later, she held out three small coins. "I put these in among Hal and Ed and Jesse," she said. "I've had them since before you were born. Your father and I went to Canada, and we kept some change when we came back, who wouldn't, to show we'd been some place. There's one that works like a dime and two that work like quarters, but it's been so long who knows if they'd buy anything now."

Stu held them. All the times he'd looked at the snakes and never noticed the coins—the snakes were like a magician's hands taking his eyes away from where the trick was taking place. "I worked them down in there pretty good," she said. "I didn't want you reaching in there like you'd found buried treasure."

"Your father was partial to telling people we'd been to a foreign country. He thought it made us special. He wanted to keep their dollars, too, but I spent them at the duty-free store right before we crossed over."

He touched the edges of each coin as if there were clues to discover about his father, and his mother smiled. "I enjoyed drinking from those Canadian bottles," she said. "It didn't seem like we'd paid anything for them using that foreign money that looked like pretend."

He laid the coins back in the tank, dropping them the last six inches as if those snakes had returned, as if he hadn't noticed they were coiled in the shadows. "I've been back to work a week now," she said.

"Good."

"Do you think I'm still attractive?" she said then, and Stu knew that no man had come back to the house with her after work that week.

"Sure."

"I'm forty-two years old, twice your age. Every one of those years means more to a woman. The girls you've been with might not know that yet, but they will."

"You're fine, Mom," he said, and when she didn't answer, his words sounded like something a doctor would say to a patient, leaving "for now" unspoken, keeping the important words to himself.

* * *

The morning radio hosts latched on to the story about a judge being dismissed from office for using a penis pump during trials. "Pump it up," the host said, and his sidekick, laughing shrilly, exclaimed, "A big, big case! Guilty as charged."

After breakfast, Stu sat with the eight pages of the front section, the ones Herrold corrected. The first two pages were almost entirely wire service articles, but on page three, Stu made the small loops for *delete* three times. He twice placed the carat for *insert* and made the horizontal parentheses of *close up space* four times. Twice he drew the parallel lines for *align*. There was a capital letter error and two en-dashes required.

Small errors, but by the time he was finished, he'd found forty-one errors. Page seven was full of syndicated columns; page eight were wire-service stories continued from pages one and two. Thirty-nine of the errors had come on the four pages that hadn't been proofed before they arrived.

After Herrold left for dinner that night, Stu tacked the four worst pages over the dog pictures surrounding Herrold's desk. Herrold would know it was Stu. Who else could do the work so well?

Stu was sure he'd be fired. Another man would have laid those pages on the editor's desk, but Stu was used to being by himself by now.

THE FIERCENESS OF NEED

"THIS KHOMENI FELLOW, what do those people over there see in him?" Sal Morrelli asked. For five minutes he'd been complaining to Ed Frank about his daughter Maria's music—"All that what they call disco. Like dancing to a song makes it something special"—but suddenly he'd switched to politics as if the late March improving weather reminded him of bad news likely to come soon from the Middle East.

"From what I've heard," Ed said, "the Shah was nasty."

Morrelli shook his head. "I don't like the looks of this guy. No matter what's happened, you can't have a church in charge of a country. There's too much hate in the people who run churches, and that one doesn't even have Jesus to calm things down."

Although he'd never been inside the place, Ed knew Morrelli ran his own restaurant. He'd passed by it a hundred times, and from the outside it looked to Ed as if Maria's hadn't changed since Morrelli opened it in 1957, six years before the daughter he'd given the same name to had been born.

Ed and his wife, Dana, had lived near Middletown, where Maria's was located, for three years without more than "Hello" from Morrelli over the fence that divided their yards. Morrelli had put the fence up years ago to keep Maria in when she was young, and now, he said, he'd gotten used to it, and maybe Ed and Dana would appreciate a fence at the end of their yard someday when they had the little ones around. But ever since Morrelli's daughter had started in Ed's class at the high school, Morrelli called him over to talk whenever he saw Ed in the yard.

Maria was in tenth grade, the *Julius Caesar* year in English. She'd finished the *Romeo and Juliet* year and had *Hamlet* and *Macbeth* to go before graduation. During Ed's three years at that high school just outside of Harrisburg, he'd taught all of those plays, and he knew it was hard doing Shakespeare in any of those years. He'd told Dana that Maria sat behind a boy who said he didn't understand anything in *Julius Caesar*, not even the lines in prose spoken by the guards. "Why?" Ed had asked him, and he'd said, "Because it's Shakespeare."

"You thinking about starting a family?" Morrelli said now, leaving the Middle East behind, abandoned like the merits of disco music, jittery, Ed thought, from the coffee he always carried into the yard in a twenty-ounce "double cup" from the local doughnut shop. "You two aren't babies anymore."

"I'm thirty," Ed said. "Dana's a few months younger."

"You don't want to be an old man when your kids need a firm hand," he said.

"One of these days soon," Ed said. He didn't want Morrelli to be the first person he told that Dana was pregnant, news she'd given him the night before, telling him to wait a few days to spread the news. "It'll be like a birthday present," she'd said, since hers was April 1st, less than a week away, but she'd looked upset, even when he hugged her. "I had two glasses of wine last night," she'd said. "I knew I shouldn't because I was late."

"It's nothing to worry about."

"Yes it is. I knew I had an appointment this afternoon. Everything matters now."

Morrelli looked across Ed's yard as if he was imagining children playing. "Look at me," he said. "I'm forty-four, and Maria's my only and about all I have the energy for."

Morrelli's daughter had dark red hair, the most beautiful hair of any girl in the school. Ed had mentioned that to Dana once, and she'd said, "That's the sort of thing you'd better keep to yourself."

"Who would I tell besides you?"

"Why am I the exception?"

"If you told me one of your fourth graders was cute," he'd said, "I wouldn't tell you to keep that to yourself," and she'd glared like her mother did every time Ed criticized Republicans.

He'd kept himself from telling her he taught twenty girls who were more attractive. He wanted to say all those girls were fifteen or sixteen, that he was twice their age, for God's sake. And he hadn't mentioned that Maria was dieting. He didn't need Dana reminding him he couldn't tell a female student who'd lost weight she was looking better, though actually, he wasn't certain she did. Instead, he remembered how his Aunt Agatha had lost weight one summer, how she'd looked like a woman he didn't know in a swimsuit, somebody to fantasize about for a few months before she pitched past that perfection to a thinness she kept under long-sleeved blouses and baggy pants.

She'd found out about the cancer before those two months of sudden beauty ended, taking six months to die. Now he watched Maria each day for whatever would tell him she was plummeting toward disaster.

* * *

The next afternoon, during his free period, Ed was reading the Wednesday *Harrisburg Patriot* in the faculty room when Will Watson, who taught history, pushed the door open and held the knob with one hand as if he expected everybody to pay attention. "You heard yet?" he said.

"What's going on?" Ed said.

Will swung the door by the knob and looked from Ed to the three other teachers sitting on the old, black, fake-leather office chairs they'd salvaged when the administration had renovated the year before. "It's not in the newspaper, that's for sure," he said.

Ed held the paper open, but he kept his eyes on Watson. "What?" he finally said.

Watson swung the door once more before he said, "Three Mile Island almost did a China Syndrome. You saw the movie, didn't you? You know what I'm talking about."

A near meltdown, Ed thought. *Almost a hole through the earth from Harrisburg to China.* Everybody in the school knew it was six miles to the atomic power plant. "There's radiation?"

"They say 'no,' but something's happened over there, you can bet on that."

The school emptied fast, the buses half full because parents who'd heard the news had already shown up in cars, the line snaking back toward Harrisburg as if it were pointing the way to the four towers on Three Mile Island. "You think we're having school tomorrow?" Ed asked Watson.

"The worst has already happened," Will said. "We're either fucked or we're fine."

Ed nodded. He'd spent the afternoon thinking that very thing about the baby Dana was carrying. By the time he arrived home, Dana, though the elementary school released a half hour later and she rode with another teacher who lived two blocks away, was already there. "Where were you?" she said.

"Blocked in by all the parents' cars."

It was a warm day, but Dana had the windows closed and the drapes pulled. "I didn't know what else to do when I got home from school," she said. "We're only seven and a half miles from that thing."

"Nothing escaped. They screwed up, but all the radioactivity was contained."

"So they say."

"Even if it wasn't, we're not at ground zero. There's thousands of people closer than us."

"My school's 6.3 miles away. Yours is closer than that. I feel like I've been kicked in the stomach."

She pointed up the stairs, and he followed her direction into the gloom. "The drapes are shut in our room," she said, "but do me a favor and close them in the guest room." He looked up the stairs a second time. "The door was already shut. I just didn't want to go in there because you can see the towers from that side of the house."

They'd planned to turn the guest room into a nursery. Dana had asked him to paint the walls a bright color and dismantle the old spare bed. He looked out the window at the towers. Men were working there right now, he thought, but there was no steam rising. The towers, which had always looked alien, looked predatory without a cloud rising from them.

"You can leave the bed in there now," Dana said when he came back downstairs. "There's the smaller extra room to make into a nursery. Let whoever visits look at those damned things, but not our child, not every morning first thing."

"We can decide that when this settles down again."

"It's decided," Dana said. "It's impossible now. Anything less than perfect is failure with your children." When he didn't answer at once, she added, "You agree, don't you?"

"There's bad luck," he said. "Heredity."

"You sound like somebody getting ready for something terrible."

"I'm realistic."

"If the baby has a problem, I won't be able to forgive myself," she said. "Or you."

* * *

Ed's students were excited the following morning. "We were on Cronkite," they said. "The lead story." When somebody during second period said if there were a hole straight through the Earth from Harrisburg, it would come out in the Indian Ocean, not China, Maria Morrelli shook her head, unfurling her beautiful red hair. "Maria?" Ed said. "You disagree?" but she stretched her thin, bare arms across her desk and didn't answer.

Dana was sitting in the dark when Ed got home. "I couldn't think straight, so I left at lunch," she said. "And so should everybody else. I've already called in sick for tomorrow. You go and kill yourself, but I'm not making our baby retarded."

She'd called her mother, who lived near Downingtown, another sixty miles farther away. "She's worried even out there," Dana said. "We're all downwind."

Ed was willing to be cautious. "We'll go there for the weekend."

"It's not just the weekend," she said. "Even my fourth graders know that by now. You should have heard them talk."

"You were scaring them."

"I was teaching them. And now I hope they all go away somewhere like I'm going to do."

By Friday morning, the students were restless again. "It's all over," they said, and Ed was happy to agree. There were jokes now, and they shared them, even the one that got the biggest laugh because it ended with a toilet and a punch line that included "nuclear waste."

But right after lunch, school was canceled, and everybody shut up and piled into buses, the closing so sudden, hardly any cars driven by parents blocked traffic. Ed nodded at Will as he crossed the parking lot, but Watson was walking fast, his head down as if he expected gunfire. As soon as he turned on the car radio, Ed heard that radiation had been released.

Dana was sitting in their bedroom with the door closed. "At least this is on the side away from the towers," she said. There were two closed suitcases on the bed. "A five mile evacuation radius for little kids and pregnant women. See? Those goddamned pricks. They waited until it was too late for everybody."

"You haven't been within five miles."

"If the governor says five, you know it should be ten. So we're going twenty."

"OK."

"From here, not from the island."

"OK," he said.

"Those pricks," Dana said again, "telling us to leave after it's too late to make a difference. I should have left the first day. Why did I listen to you and wait for the governor to say it wasn't safe?"

"I'll fill one of those as fast as I can," he said, but Dana walked past him through the door.

"We're all packed," she said. "Just carry everything down. If I had a car, I wouldn't even be here."

"I understand," Ed said, but she was already on her way down the stairs.

***

The turnpike entrance was less than five minutes away, a twenty-car line at every ticket booth. As they started and stopped, Dana hunched forward, looking through the windshield toward the towers as if she expected an explosion. "Finally," she said as Ed accelerated onto the highway, and he was quick to say, "We're out of it."

Dana snorted. "Hardly," she said, and settled into calling out each of the mileage markers along the turnpike. Ed noted that a few of the trees showed green. The warm weather had brought out early leaves. In a couple of weeks, they'd all be green, and it wouldn't matter which had been first, but at this time of year he'd never been able to tell one from another. It was easier to tell later in the year—oak had acorns, maple had the helicopter seeds. And weren't the elms all dead now, killed by some blight around the time he'd been born?

When they passed the twentieth one, she relaxed. "Good," Dana said, and though she didn't explain, he could do the math and knew they were nearly thirty miles from the reactor now, a radius that seemed to signal safety to Dana. The next exit was two more miles. They'd be twenty-five miles from the evacuation zone.

Dana drew the drapes in their motel room and turned on the news. Some radiation had been released, the newscaster said, but not for long, and the episode had ended. Dana smiled grimly. "The episode," she said. "Like we're supposed to tune in next week."

"I'm starving," Ed said.

"I'm staying inside. Order a pizza. I don't want you out there either."

"I'll be driving back in on Monday. The school won't close unless something worse happens."

"Like what? A mushroom cloud? We're calling in sick."

"You can, but not me. I'm not pregnant."

They stayed inside, had pizza and Chinese delivered, then hoagies and pizza again, watching movies and the news. They learned that the president had visited Three Mile Island, that the governor accompanied him. Ed lay back on the bed and felt himself begin to relax. "That's better," he said. "You know it has to be safe because those two aren't going to stick their necks out like martyrs."

Dana stayed in the chair where she'd been sitting close to the television. "I don't know what they're up to, but this motel isn't crowded enough to suit me. If there are rooms available it means we're still too close."

* * *

Driving under the speed limit the whole way, Ed went back to school Monday, the news on the half hour, all of it vague and ambivalent, repeating itself before he arrived. More than a third of the students were absent. "A landslide for panic," said Will Watson, who seemed assured again. "If this was an election, this would be a mandate."

Ed was pleased to have no more than sixteen students in any of his classes, in two classes as few as ten. "What's done is done," said the boy who didn't understand Shakespeare. He lived closer to the towers than anyone in the room. Maria Morrelli, sitting in front of him, shifted in her chair by the minute, as jittery as her father.

In every class, Ed allowed them to talk about Three Mile Island. The students told stories about how they'd all stayed home and talked to their parents through the weekend the way they had when they were little. It was the most interesting day of school they'd had all year, and in his enthusiasm, Ed asked all of them to write their stories down and bring them in the following day just to have them to keep.

Morrelli was outside when Ed took the garbage out for the Tuesday morning pickup. "Jimmy Carter's either braver than I ever gave him credit for, or he's the biggest fool in the world," Morrelli said.

"Both," Ed said, but Morrelli's expression didn't change. "Dana's upset because she's pregnant."

Morrelli smiled. "Is she now? That's good news." He lit a cigarette, and for a minute Ed thought he was going to pass it over the fence in celebration.

"She won't come home or go to work since the meltdown."

"She can quit then. She can just tell them she's done with it. It's April already."

"There's maternity leave, but she'd have to have a medical emergency to start that already. She thinks I'm crazy going to school this week. If you asked her your question about dying, she'd tell you we're killing ourselves just standing here outside."

"Nobody's died yet," Morrelli said.

Ed shook his head. "By the time they do, nobody but their families will notice."

* * *

When Ed collected the essays the next day, almost half the students in each class hadn't finished them. "We thought they were for fun," they said, and when he agreed, they answered, "Exactly." The students who returned, swelling the classes near capacity, talked among themselves as if it were the first day of school.

"School sucks again," somebody said during second period, and he nodded without thinking, calling up laughter from the class of

10th graders where Maria Morrelli sat looking at her arms and legs, glancing down at her chest as if she'd scattered crumbs on herself.

Dana's mother was at the motel when he arrived. "We're still too close here. They're all lying. That's what the government does."

"If it's a problem here, the country has bigger headaches than you can imagine."

"Maybe it does. I bet if you go up on a hill you can see those damned towers."

"Through a telescope," he said.

"Is that supposed to be funny?" She glanced toward the window, then glared at him. "Are there jokes already about radioactivity? I'll bet there are."

Ed thought of the poop joke his students had told, but said, "They're remaking *Attack of the 50 Foot Woman*. She's going to tear down Harrisburg."

"Whatever are you talking about?"

He felt as if he were being smothered by a thick, feather-filled pillow, the kind he hadn't used since he was five and the allergist had forbidden them. "Wait until the cancer starts. Wait until the babies have webbed feet and hare lips and their hearts outside of their bodies."

"Dana's fine. The baby's fine."

"You sound like a priest," she said. "Like someone who's never going to have a wife and children so he doesn't have a care in the world."

* * *

Will Watson's wife taught in the elementary school where Dana did. "It's been over a week," Will said on Friday, "and Amy says Dana hasn't come back. They have a sub in for her who lets the kids get away with murder."

"Dana's pregnant," he said. "She's concerned. The school's seven miles from the island, but she doesn't want to be the 'next closest' pregnant woman."

Will brightened. "Hey, congratulations, welcome to being poor. Amy and I never caught up after the three years she missed with Will, Jr. and Annie."

"Yeah. That, too."

"But she might as well finish the year. There's only about a mile from your house to the grade school. That doesn't make any difference."

The mail had piled up on the dining room table, all of it untouched. The refrigerator was empty except for condiments and salad dressings. The open baking soda box Dana used to keep odors away stood exposed on an empty shelf. He hadn't opened the drapes. It looked like the house of people on a long vacation. A house that might be robbed. "We'll see," he said.

Will would tell Amy the news, and it would spread. For a few more days, everybody would think Dana was being sensible to be cautious. Until somebody stopped in and learned she was gone, that she'd evacuated permanently like a flood victim whose house had slid from its foundation.

* * *

As he did every afternoon at four, Ed called the motel, but now there was a message from Dana that she'd gone to her mother's, another thirty-five miles, almost to Philadelphia. "There's talk that everybody will be told to come back soon," he said when Dana's mother answered the phone.

"You come out here now and be with your wife. Even if they say it's safe to come back, you know it's not true."

"I can't do that. I can't drive over an hour to work every day."

"You can live with us in Downingtown until you find a new job," she said. "There's no going back to that house of yours where it's sitting."

"Sure there is. A bomb didn't go off."

"That's what you think. You'll be lucky anybody takes it off your hands."

Who's selling? he thought. He opened the American Literature anthology he used in two of his classes, flipping through the pages while she went on, her voice so loud he could lay the receiver on the shelf that held cookbooks and wait for a pause. The classes had reached Stephen Crane and "The Open Boat." The last two months of American Literature were set in the twentieth century. When he picked up the phone, he heard, "Dana's been a mother for three months now. A man's like that disciple in the Bible, he has to see the baby for himself before he becomes a father."

"It's almost certainly safe here," Ed said.

"Almost? If it's not, a million people will have cancer. Here, you tell your wife 'almost' and see how she feels about that."

Ed closed the book and stood up as Dana took the phone. "I'm never going back," Dana said at once. "Not ever. Not when the baby's born. Not when it's growing up and becoming a child."

"I'm finishing the year at school."

"OK." Her tone frightened him. It sounded as if he were already abandoned, that she expected him to die.

"We have to work this out in June."

"I'll be here," she said. "They can keep their job. Get somebody who doesn't have kids teach right there in the shadow of the damn thing."

"In June," he said. *Sylvia Plath. Ralph Ellison. John Updike.*

"You think you're being brave staying home?" she said.

"I think I'm being sensible."

"You keep thinking that way then because not leaving the house is as far from brave as you can get."

By eight o'clock, the light barely out of the sky, Ed lay in bed, not sinking toward the center where he and Dana would always converge on the cheap mattress. Without her body beside him, he simply sank into his side, and it felt awkward, like trying to sleep in a hammock. He turned into the middle of the bed, faced Dana's side, and there was such a longing in him that he pressed his lips together to keep from whimpering out loud like an old dog.

* * *

Dana's mother greeted him on Saturday. "They say 140,000 people left the Harrisburg area. You can't tell me they all live within five miles."

He thought Dana was quiet because the governor had invited small children and pregnant women back home, but her mother rattled on while she made dinner. When it was served, Dana said, "Please, Mom, enough," and for a minute the table was so quiet it felt as if everyone had left the room.

"Well," Dana's mother said to Ed at last, "Have you seen those newsreels from Iran? All those people packed together and cheering for that priest?"

"The Ayatollah."

"Is that what those people call their priests? They should know better. It's just like us trusting Jimmy Carter or that governor of ours. No different at all. Any time a big bunch of people trust one person something terrible happens."

"Mother," Dana said, "you promised." And to Ed's relief, dinner was finished without one more word.

By ten o'clock, Ed was the only one awake. He flipped through channels until 11:30, waiting for *Saturday Night Live*. The lead skit took place in an atomic power plant on Two Mile Island. Ed sat up and leaned forward when the soda spilled on the controls and the alarms went off. "The Pepsi Syndrome"—the audience laughed, as Dan Ackroyd, playing Jimmy Carter, exposed himself to radiation and turned huge like one of those spiders or ants or lizards from old movies. The Amazing Colossal President. His students would be watching. They'd recount the skit for him on Monday, laughing like the audience.

The next morning Ed was relieved when Dana suggested a walk. "I'm not crazy," she said. "I can go outside here."

She turned left, and Ed followed. The neighborhood stayed up-scale, the yards immaculate and green even after ten minutes of walking in a straight line. Eight blocks, he counted, a half mile of wealth and at least another block to come. You could believe that nobody had a defective child on streets like these.

"Don't you feel better here?" Dana said.

"Because we're seventy-five miles from Harrisburg?"

"You know what I mean. It's nicer here. The schools have to be better."

He felt bitterness churn up his throat, the thick pancakes and syrup of breakfast becoming unsettled. "Do they have special ed?" he said.

Her hands cupped her stomach as if they expected a bulge. "You don't know how awful you sound."

"Yes, I do."

"Then it's unforgivable."

"So what do you think now that Thornburgh says it's OK for everybody?" he said, but Dana had turned and headed back, still holding her stomach with her hands.

* * *

Ed's students were less attentive the following week, enough of them whispering to each other that their collective voice was audible. Soon they would be talking out loud, and his classes would crumble like the ones you could hear in the halls even with their doors closed, like the cafeteria or the school bus, so many conversations that the voices amplified as if they were fueled by alcohol. One evening, when he watched *The Incredible Shrinking Man* on television for something to do, Ed believed that the movie had it right not to make radiation victims larger, even when the shrinking man was nearly gone by the end of the movie. There wasn't a limit to disappearing. He felt smaller, even his voice reduced somehow in a way that his students sensed.

The next night, when he saw an ambulance outside of Morrelli's at midnight, he thought Sal had had a heart attack from all of those cigarettes and cups of coffee. His students told him first thing in the morning. Maria Morrelli had been in that ambulance. She'd had some sort of seizure and was in the hospital.

After school, Ed sat in Maria's desk. He didn't know one other student who'd starved herself into the hospital. Instead, he remembered Patty Worthington, who'd sat in front of him in tenth grade history, how she'd gotten pregnant and left school, the only girl he'd known like that. Which couldn't possibly be true—the only reason he didn't know a dozen more was secrecy.

Now girls in his senior class seemed proud of being pregnant. They were sure to graduate, finished with school. Only the sophomores and juniors cried at the news, not because they were embarrassed, but because they would miss football games and dances.

He looked toward where he usually stood. All of the pictures of authors and displays of student essays were on bulletin boards behind Maria's chair and to her right. His desk was bare; the blackboard was empty. Looking forward, there was nothing in the room that distinguished it from any other room except that he, instead of another teacher, stood in front of the students.

Or who filled the other desks, he thought at once, knowing it was foolish to sit there without the room being packed with students.

* * *

Saturday morning, before he left for Downingtown, Ed knocked on Morrelli's door. His wife answered, a near stranger. "Come in," she said. "Sal's in a tizzy, but he has a minute." Ed had never been inside Morrelli's house, but he noticed at once that everything looked like it belonged to a husband and wife who were a generation older—the Last Supper print, the wicker rocking chair, the sewing machine in one corner of the living room. "It turns out you can get so skinny you can die," she said. "Who would have thought?"

"Anorexia," Morrelli said, entering the room empty-handed. He looked different without a cigarette or a cup of coffee.

"That's what they call it," his wife said, "but she's going to live."

"For now," Morrelli said, calling up a shortness of breath in Ed. "She's in Harrisburg. They have to fatten her up, of all things. Like those kids in that story where the witch ends up in the oven."

"Dana's living in Downingtown," Ed said. "She doesn't believe we're not crazy."

Morrelli nodded, as if he already knew. "Ellen's got business of her own with a doctor in Hershey. That's what we were working on when you knocked."

"I'll give you a lift," Ed said. He could spare an hour or two, miss at least one lecture by Dana's mother.

"Thank you," Morrelli said as they settled into Ed's car. As soon as Ed twisted the ignition, the Bee Gees leaped out of the dashboard speakers, singing "Stayin' Alive." Ed reached to turn the radio down, but Morrelli waved him off. "That's those fellows Maria's always listening to," Morrelli said. "Those squeaky guys."

Ed entered the highway as "Night Fever" came on. "A block of the Bee Gees," the announcer said. "Four in a row."

"Are they that popular?" Morrelli said. "Why?"

"There's ten million girls like Maria who love them," Ed said.

"How many you think are starving themselves?"

"I don't know. None, I hope."

"I hope there's a few, at least," Morrelli said. "Or else I'll know it's all my fault."

*　*　*

While Morrelli visited, Ed walked along the river that ran across the street from the hospital. The scenic path was used by joggers and mothers with small children in strollers. A few of them were visibly pregnant. Ed knew there were newborn babies in that hospital, doctors dealing with them with confidence. By now Dana would be expecting him, and he wondered if she would turn anxious, moving to the window and staying there while her mother blathered on about a world full of threats.

Morrelli had told him Maria was on the top floor. "The penthouse," he'd called it, and Ed looked at the highest sets of windows where Morrelli might be standing. He thought of waving, a surprise for Morrelli if he were there, his back to his bedridden daughter.

Instead, he crossed the street and rode the elevator to the top floor, found a magazine, and sat down to wait.

He read for fifteen minutes before Morrelli stepped through one of the three sets of swinging doors to the reception area. Morrelli didn't invite him down the hall to see Maria, but he gestured toward that door as if an entire wing of the hospital were full of skeletal girls. "They say there's no telling with this," he said. "I think it's like being a drunk. You know."

"Really?" He didn't want to tell Morrelli he wasn't convinced alcoholism was a disease. If you brought it on yourself, he thought, it was a weakness—like overeating, like smoking. Dana had told him for years that he was wrong, that "studies proved," what she always said to back up her arguments, but even now he was tempted to say, "Just make her clean her plate," and wanted Morrelli to answer, "You bet I will."

Morrelli shuffled over to a window, and when Ed followed, he noticed the towers at once, visible from the top floor of the hospital. "We're almost on the other side of them now," Ed said, "but they look exactly the same from every angle."

"Like hell does," Morrelli said, and he slid what looked to be an old snapshot toward him. "You see this here?" The face in the photo was a stranger's, but Ed knew Morrelli meant him to look again, that he was supposed to recognize someone.

And he did. It was Morrelli. Younger, of course, but fatter. Maybe a hundred pounds fatter. A pumpkin head on Tweedledee's body.

"Cigarettes and coffee," Morrelli said. "And staying on my feet all day. I don't give myself time to do anything but work."

Ed looked at the back of the photo to see if it was dated, but there was nothing written there. "1963," Morrelli said. "When Joan told me she was pregnant with Maria. I had her take this picture because

I knew I couldn't let the child we'd been trying to have for six years see me that way. I shut my fat mouth and got busy." He slid the photo back into his wallet. "Tell you what. Let me make you a hot turkey sandwich and a milkshake at my place. As a thank you. It's not far. By then the wife will be here."

This time, before he started the car, Ed turned off the radio. They drove back toward the towers, neither of them saying anything about the distance, even when they parked outside of Maria's, closer to the accident site than Ed had been since the incident.

He watched Morrelli scoop ice cream into the kind of metal shake cup he hadn't seen in ten years. While Morrelli poured milk from a carton and added syrup, Ed noticed that the glass that would hold his shake had an A' embossed on it. Above Morrelli's head were dozens of similar glasses, and Ed noted several each of R, M, I, A, and S. Morrelli held up the A' glass before he poured the shake. "If there's a table with six customers, they get the full name every time, and when it's only two or four, we make sure they don't get duplicates." Morrelli tapped Ed's glass. "Some think this A with the apostrophe is rare, and they ask for it special."

The sandwich was wonderful. Three slices of white meat off the bone over a thick slab of whole wheat bread with gravy that wasn't from a can. Ed thought of the "family restaurant" franchises along the road to Harrisburg, the chances that any of them served food this good. "Thank you," he said.

"There's all these places now," Morrelli said. "You know the places I mean, all of them the same and sprouting up all over like dandelions."

"People know it's different here. They'll come back after they try the other places."

"You see them?" Morrelli said. Ed could count seven people in the restaurant, three at the counter, and one table with four. He looked away before Morrelli would think he was counting the empty tables, but he knew there were thirty, maybe more.

* * *

A half hour later Ed waited once more while Morrelli went down to the hospital room. "Only a minute," Morrelli said, so Ed didn't pick up a magazine. He crossed one leg over the other and looked around the room, which was empty except for a young girl, maybe seven or eight, with her mother.

It took ten minutes, but Morrelli reappeared, extending his hand. "The wife is here," he said. "I have a ride. Now go to that wife of yours. It's just need she feels; it's not being loony. There's something fierce in all of us that sometimes gets touched."

When Ed let go of Morrelli's hand, he noticed that the girl was alone. *How had he missed the mother leaving?* "Probably," he said.

"There's no probably in this, let me tell you."

"I loved the lunch," Ed said, but Morrelli waved him off and disappeared down the hall, the door going still after three diminishing arcs. When Ed turned, the girl was standing beside him. She handed him a piece of paper. "I drew you," she said, and he inspected a picture of a square-shouldered man with no neck and arms to the side like a muscle-bound weight lifter. The face, though, was detailed. A realistic nose, eyes in proportion, an expressive mouth. It was as if the girl had taken art lessons that began with the human face.

"I look sad," he said.

She smiled. "Yes," she said. "I thought so. You can keep it if you give me a dollar."

"That's expensive."

"It's not for candy. It's for college."

"Oh? OK." He opened his wallet and gave the girl a dollar just as he noticed the girl's mother reappear through the same door Morrelli had used. He wanted to explain, but the girl tucked the dollar into her pocket. "I won't tell," she said, the words giving him a sudden chill.

He didn't fold the picture. He carried it by one corner and laid it on the passenger seat like a map, but instead of heading toward the turnpike, Ed drove downriver until he was across from the towers. He knew the area along this shore was called Goldsboro, and he stood beside his car, about as close, he thought, as someone without authority could get to the power plant. He'd never gotten over how huge cooling towers were. Surely someone had compared them to pyramids. If there weren't so many of them, they'd be wonders.

He caught himself taking shallow breaths. He took his hands from his pockets and stood straighter, opening his lungs to the full breaths of the diving board or the free throw line. *You can learn to live with anything,* he thought.

He inhaled slowly. Steadied himself. It would take years to prove anything. Like the location of paradise, he thought, ready to get in the car and drive, but making himself stand there breathing deeply, teaching himself to hope.

WEEPERS

EARLY IN THE SUMMER of my twelfth birthday, when my mother found me lying at the bottom of the stairs to the basement, my feet three steps up as if I'd fallen and broken my neck, I vowed to stop pretending I was dead. My mother agreed. "If I find you like this again," she said, "I'm taking you to see somebody."

She'd told me to stop a month before when she'd seen me lying on the cellar floor. That time she'd let out a gasp that made me pull my legs and arms in tight against my body. "You gave me a fright," she'd said. "You're too old for that."

I didn't want to see whoever that "somebody" was, so I stopped playing dead in the house, but I had other secrets, some of them worse. Jerking off, for one. Taking sips of our neighbor June Hutka's drinks, for another. I wanted to own a glass like the one she used for those drinks, keeping it nearby in the afternoons. Thick and squat, it was heavy like the ashtray that sat on the circular wooden table that filled half the Hutkas' back porch from April to October. My family owned plastic tumblers, old jelly jars, and a set of four glasses frosted with a tulip design that we used for holiday meals, the ones that were celebrated indoors like Easter, Thanksgiving, and Christmas. Besides water and coffee, my parents drank ginger ale and root beer that they shared with me and my younger sister on Saturdays. "Fancy glasses are for drinkers," my mother said more than once as she handed us root beer in plastic cups. My sister Jackie was nine. She was happy to have root beer even if it came in a paper cup.

"They like their drink over there at the Hutkas'," my father would add, and that was the end of that.

Best of all, June Hutka's glass clinked every time she picked it up, ice cubes swirling into its sides, nothing like the dull thunk of ice against our plastic cups. In the morning she carried a mug of coffee, always a black one with Atlantic City stenciled on one side, but in the afternoon, even when the weather turned hot and muggy, there always seemed to be fresh ice in her glass while she lay in the sun to darken her tan, sitting up only to smoke and drink from that glass.

June Hutka had a record player that looked like a suitcase. For three straight sunny days, I sat on the grass where our backyards touched and listened to an hour of the songs on her records until, the third afternoon, June waved me to her porch and told me to help myself to one of the bottles of ginger ale that was half buried in ice inside the small cooler tucked into the shade made by the table. She had me drop two cubes into her nearly empty glass, had me pour a few splashes of ginger ale into it, and then she topped it off from a bottle labeled Four Roses.

I'd never seen a whiskey bottle. I picked it up and held it to the light. "You don't want to take it straight from the bottle," she said. "And your mother would have my hide."

"Sorry," I said.

"Don't be sorry. Here, take a little sip of this so you don't have to be imagining what it tastes like."

I made sure I didn't act as if it burned all the way down. "I'm impressed," June said. "I thought your parents were teetotalers."

She sounded like my mother, who was always giving me big

words to look up in the dictionary. I took a second sip, kept my expression fixed, and handed the glass back to her. I'd never heard that word before, but it sounded like something I wished my parents weren't.

What I noticed that afternoon was her records were all 78s, which, in 1957, were hardly ever in stores anymore. Some kids my age had stacks of 45s, but nobody I knew owned records like the ones she played. All of the songs sounded as if the singer were more than sad, as if he were in misery. "They're all weepers, Georgie," she told me that day while I sipped ginger ale on her porch. "It's what breaks our hearts."

I nodded and watched her 78s spin. I loved seeing the grooves spiral into the center because it looked as if the record were unraveling, that the tight circles unwound and then somehow reformed by going under the label and reappearing back at the beginning, something like the fountain in the showroom of Mertz Chevrolet, which never ran out of water though it spilled over three layers of polished metal that reminded me of a wedding cake.

June Hutka laughed when I told her that, and then she rumpled my hair. She lifted the arm from the record that was about to end, took the record off the turntable, and let me slip the next one into place, making sure I held it by the edge as I centered it over the little knob that kept it from spinning away like a flying saucer. "Leave that thing on top off to the side so it keeps playing for a while," she said, pointing to the spindle meant to hold several records in place until they dropped, one by one, and played. That afternoon the song I put on for her was called "Cry."

"Listen to that man sing, Georgie," she said. "You can tell he's a heartbreaker." I watched the record spin until the song ended and the arm lifted, returning automatically to where the record began. "Johnny Ray," she nearly whispered in the same voice I imagined a girl using to say my name. Johnny Ray sounded heartbroken himself. He sang the word *cry* over and over, and I thought he was ready to cry out loud right there in the middle of the song. "See there?" June said, and I looked at that record spinning as if Johnny Ray could walk out of it and break her heart by weeping.

"I think he's on his way out, Georgie," she said. "I think maybe the world is tired of weepers."

My mother never turned on the radio. She was listening to me and my sister, she said. She needed the air to be clear. My father's old record player was in the basement on the floor beside a musty-smelling blue couch. Nobody had played his old 78s since we'd moved into the house when I was in second grade.

June Hutka, on the other hand, didn't have any kids to worry about. She had a husband named Bud, who I hardly ever saw except on weekends because he was a travelling salesman. But when he was there, he looked just like her, a cigarette and a drink close by while he worked in the yard, always without a shirt on so he could keep up with his own deep tan. She told me he was twenty-seven years old, ten years younger than my father.

Bud Hutka, when he was home, never seemed to leave his house and yard. The car stayed in the driveway day and night. "He has some sense about himself, at least," my mother said, "not like that wife of his showing herself to the world every day like a floozy." She huffed a bit and made the face she used when she caught me picking my nose. A floozy was what June Hutka would be if she weren't married, my mother explained. "And that's all you need to know until you're old enough." I kept to myself that floozies were what I imagined twice a day when I locked myself in the bathroom to jerk off. And I didn't complain because she and my father were teetotalers who would hate June Hutka for letting me sip her drink.

"And her poor husband, a vet like your father."

My mother thought surviving a war amplified good qualities a man might have, and, at least for a time, was an excuse for any mistakes a man might make. "It's hard to settle down after," she said. "You didn't know your father back before you were born." Bud was a Korean War vet. My father had made it from North Africa to Italy, surviving a year in combat before he was sent home with a wound that kept him from turning his head. "He won't talk about it," my mother said every few months, as if being secretive were a character strength the war had promoted.

I didn't care what my mother said about June Hutka. I loved talking to her. Like her husband, I never wore a shirt outside, though by the middle of June I was always picking at the skin on my shoulders where I was peeling, because as soon as school was over, I'd laid out in the sun until I got my annual sunburn. My back was more sunburned than my chest because I didn't have sunglasses, and it was hard keeping my eyes shut against the sun. When I played dead, I could sprawl, but lying stiff on a blanket with my arms at my sides, every noise made me anxious, so I'd open them, squint, and roll back over to my stomach.

It didn't much matter because I stayed out so long I was burned on my chest and stomach, too. "You look like the devil's apprentice," June had said the week before. "One of his elves." I liked her calling me that and checked the mirror for an hour or two after I went inside because I always got redder for a while longer. "The devil's elf," I said to myself, and I slid my shorts down a few inches, astonished at how pale the rest of me was, imagining how white June looked under her two-piece suits.

For a day or two it hurt to have a shirt on, but sunburn was no worse than throwing up from the flu. After that I just itched and began to lose a layer of skin. "You're peeling like all get out," June said when she noticed me picking. "You're like a snake shedding its skin. It's like you're growing and need more room for all those muscles that are coming."

"I like being tan."

"Don't we all, sugar." She pointed to a brown bottle with a smiling sun on the label. "But when women get to be my age they have to slather on stuff like that to keep their skin in one piece."

"Why?"

"Just you wait. The answer will walk right up and whisper itself in your ear. Trust me, you'll hear it."

I didn't tell her that I loved tugging pieces of myself off my shoulders and chest. That I held up the larger bits to see how the light shone through them because they were so thin. Underneath I looked new, a shade of red that would darken on its way to brown.

What else I never told June was that my father had made it clear that if you weren't tan by the end of June, you wore your sissyhood right there on your body, a boy who kept his shirt on or worse, a boy who spent all of his time inside. Peeling was what boys did, as natural as throwing a baseball. That was the last summer I was eligible for Little League, and every boy on my team had a sunburn that peeled, like mine, by the second week of summer vacation.

None of my teammates lived near me. The only boy close to my age who lived on our short street of twelve houses was Paul Kagle, who was a year older and lived two houses away. His father worked for the state liquor control board. "He likes his drink, too," my father said, and that seemed accurate, because Mr. Kagle had a collection of shot glasses in his den that Paul liked to pick up and pretend to drink from, throwing his head back like he was letting water run on his face in the shower. All of them were made of the same thick glass as June Hutka's.

Every other boy near my age who lived within half a mile lived in the new housing project that began where the backyards on our side of the street ended. Those boys, all of the ones who'd moved into the small, nearly identical houses since the summer before, never took off their shirts, but they didn't look like sissies. They had ways to make their arms and shoulders bigger. For starters, they smoked. And they said "fuck you" to each other like "hello."

We'd moved three years earlier, my mother said, "to get away from that element." One of them, my mother said, had been in reform school. "Wayne Cook," she said. "You stay clear of him. He's fourteen going on prison." Paul Kagle, from his upstairs window, had pointed out Wayne Cook as he leaned against a car talking to two other boys in the driveway of the house behind Paul's. Wayne Cook and those other boys all had haircuts that looked like James Dean's in *Rebel Without a Cause*. "Lucky Strikes," Paul said. "They all smoke Lucky Strikes. You can tell by the target on their cigarette packs."

One Saturday afternoon near the end of June, I saw Wayne Cook and those other two other boys smoking in the yard behind the Hutkas'. Lucky Strikes, I remembered, but I couldn't see any packs to make sure. The two boys whose names I didn't know held their cigarettes alongside their bodies, arms extended, but Wayne Cook held his burning cigarette in front of his chest near his heart until he lifted it to his mouth. He looked so cool I was sure he'd stood in front of the mirror to practice.

Suddenly, Bud Hutka put aside his hedge clippers, walked toward the end of his yard and shouted "fuck off" to Wayne Cook and the others. Cook grinned, but he and the others backed away slowly, all of them taking a drag on their cigarettes before they turned and walked away. "Jesus Christ, June," Bud said to his wife. She was wearing an all white two-piece bathing suit I'd never seen before and lying, for once, on a blanket in the back yard, nothing playing on her record player. I was glad my mother wasn't around because I knew what he meant and was happy she didn't do anything but sit up, take a drink, and lie back down again.

Paul Kagle had magazines to look at that were filled with pictures of naked women who had their crotches and nipples covered by small black bars. He kept them hidden behind a set of encyclopedias his mother had bought with coupons at the grocery store, adding one each month for a year until she had the whole collection. "Look at her tits," he said every time, shoving the magazine toward me. "Just look at them."

I looked.

"They look just like old lady Hutka's," he said.

I looked again and imagined June's face on that body. Now, watching her laying out in that white suit, I tried to imagine the rest of her breasts but saw only those black bars.

* * *

"Hey," Bud Hutka said to me the following Saturday when he noticed me hanging around his porch. "You still play soldier with that boy from up the street?"

"No," I said, glad that he hadn't said "fuck off" to me.

He finished what was left of his drink and cocked his head, looking as if he were sizing me up. "I guess you're too old for that now. What are you—eleven, twelve?"

"Twelve," I said, though my birthday was a week away. I knew what he was talking about. The summer before I'd been playing soldier with Paul Kagle at the construction sites behind our side of the street. After Paul had gone inside for lunch, I practiced being killed, tumbling down the piles of dirt. I was just trying to learn what it would feel like to fall as if I'd been shot dead. The main thing was to drop to the ground without throwing out my hands like somebody who was alive, and I could barely manage flopping backwards with my feet already on the ground. I knew all the places where men like my uncles had died. Bataan. Omaha Beach. Guadalcanal. I'd seen *Sands of Iwo Jima* twice, once with my mother and once with my Great-Uncle Willy, who'd fought in World War I and come back in one piece. "When men die, they don't act like they do in these movies," he'd said. "They fall like a sack of potatoes."

After I'd fallen, I stayed down, sprawled on my stomach in the dirt at the base of one mound, playing dead. I lay there for a minute, holding my breath. I felt something crawl across my arm and didn't move until I felt a shoe nudge my shoulder. I opened my eyes and saw Bud standing over me. "You're making a fool of yourself," was all he said. It was the last time I played soldier.

Now, with his wife watching us, Bud made a fresh drink while he kept his eyes on me. "It doesn't matter how old you are," he said at last. "They'll be a war for you, count on it."

"Bud," June said. She picked up her drink, the half-melted ice cubes still clinking against the glass.

"It's the truth. There's a war for every boy when his time comes." Bud looked angry. He looked like somebody who'd taken his shirt off so it wouldn't get torn when he started to fight.

"My mom says if I go to college I won't have to fight." The words sounded weak as soon as I said them.

"Does she now? Did she explain how you could be a fairy and not fight, too?"

"Bud," June said again.

Bud gave her a look, and then he smiled. "The boy's eyes show he's red-blooded. I'll vouch for that." The way he said it made me blush, and Bud gave me a soft punch on the shoulder. "Should I be worried?" he said, and then he flicked a piece of my dead, peeling skin off my arm. "You know how you can tell a snake's healthy even though you can't see it?" he said.

"No."

"The skin it's shed is all in one piece. If it's all in pieces, something's wrong."

"It's hard to settle down after," June said after he walked away to finish cutting the grass. I felt chilled hearing her repeat my mother's line. It sounded like a lie. The war had been over for almost four years, which seemed like a long time to settle, and I was afraid I knew why he didn't mind me staring at his wife when he acted like those project boys were criminals for looking.

* * *

In mid-July, my mother gave me a record player a week after my birthday. "I had to save up another book of Green Stamps," she explained, and she gave me five dollars to start my collection. The first record I bought was a 45, "Whispering Bells," by the Del Vikings. I brought it home in a bag with records by Elvis, Paul Anka, and Dion & The Belmonts.

When we got out of the car, my mother pointed at the two paper sacks of bottles that were sitting alongside the Hutkas' big metal garbage can. "Look at that," she said. "Who knows what they'll leave out next?" She shook one of the bags and looked inside as if she wanted to read the labels. "Trouble's coming," she said.

My mother tried to close the bags, but they were too stuffed. "You know what discretion means?" she said, and I shook my head. "You make sure you find out," she said, but I was looking past her to where June Hutka, dressed in blue shorts and a red halter top, was approaching with another bag of bottles.

"Cleaning house," she said cheerfully.

When my mother didn't answer, I held up my bag and said, "I'm starting my own collection, but none of them are weepers."

"You're too young for that," she said, dropping the bag and patting me on the head. "If they're still around, you'll bring some home in a few years. Once you start chasing, you'll learn."

My mother made a sound like "ssssssttt," and June smiled.

"Heartbreakers," she said. "It's in them all."

"Let's hope not," my mother said, already moving toward the front door.

"It's what makes the world go round," June called after her.

"That Bud Hutka, he's one that'll never grow up," my mother said after I followed her inside. "She's just studying on what's coming. Sooner or later he'll be another one that's flown the coop." I thought maybe she was going to say that his time was up for settling, that there was some sort of limit and Bud had reached it, but she didn't say another word. Half an hour later she shut my bedroom door after I'd let "Whispering Bells" play five consecutive times. I slipped the record back into its paper sleeve and put on Paul Anka. I'd heard he was only sixteen years old. "I'm so young and you're so old," he sang to Diana as if it barely mattered, but I let it play until my mother shouted, "Enough's enough" through the closed door.

* * *

The next afternoon June Hutka let a song called "Glory of Love" play over and over. "That's so poignant," she said as it started again. "Poignant. You know that word, Georgie?"

"Yeah," I lied.

"So you know it's sadder than sad," she said, which was why, besides being in love with her perfect breasts, I liked June. She didn't embarrass me by pouncing on my weaknesses. "Don't you always go around believing there's a better life you're missing out on?"

"Sometimes," I said, which didn't seem like a lie at all, because right then I realized my longing for a different life and my addiction to masturbation had arrived simultaneously just after Christmas, when I'd fallen into a funk, disappointed by every gift because not one of them had been anything but new clothes. I'd told myself the combination of bad weather, no new board games, and no record player had driven me to the pleasure of jerking off twice a day, looking forward to it like my next McDonald's hamburgers and fries. I liked it, but it was sadder than sad. Now I had an important sounding name for it.

"Those songs Mrs. Hutka plays are so poignant," I told my mother that evening.

"That's some vocabulary," she said, and I began to pick at the last piece of dead skin just above the waistband of my shorts. She watched me for a few seconds, and then my mother, who wanted me to be a doctor, had me look up *desquamation*, which turned out to be the real word for peeling. "Now you have a head start for your first test about the skin," she said.

* * *

Paul Kagle wanted me to see where a boy named Roy Gillner lived. "A real hood," he said, though he didn't say anything about him being in reform school. "The toughest hood in junior high school." I was shirtless, but he was wearing a striped polo shirt and khaki Bermuda shorts. I was beginning to worry what junior high might do to me. Wayne Cook and Roy Gillner and all of the rest were hardly older than we were. And after all, the fathers on the streets where hoods lived cut the grass in their tiny yards just like our fathers. Barking dogs were the same no matter where they lived. They didn't attack anybody who was walking in the middle of the street.

The first kids we walked by were all smaller than us, and none of them looked like they'd turn into hoods. I heard "Whispering Bells" start up from behind one of the screen doors. Paul said, "It's the Del Vikings," as if I needed to be reminded, and I wondered if he knew part of the group was black, something I'd read in one of the magazines my sister brought home from houses where her friends had older sisters.

I didn't answer, but I stopped to listen to that song I'd played about a hundred times already. I drifted one step up the walk toward the door, getting closer to the Del Vikings until the screen door swung open. "Roy Gillner," I heard Paul whisper, but I was looking inside where a girl was dancing to the Del Vikings, her hips jerking in the shadows. She didn't look as if she cared whether or not Roy Gillner was dancing with her.

"Hey fairies, you lost?" Roy Gillner said.

Paul said, "Let's go, Sutkins."

Roy Gillner laughed. "That's right, suck yunz. You two fly off where the fairies go."

I said, "Good tune," and tried to turn in a way that looked casual. I walked toward Paul, trying to read his eyes for a sign that Gillner was coming up from behind. I didn't want to get any messages, and when I didn't receive any except the Del Vikings fading away and the screen door slamming, I was giddy enough to turn and look back like I wasn't in any hurry, but there was nothing but an empty yard.

* * *

Near the end of July, Bud called me inside his house when he noticed me drinking from a bottle of ginger ale on the porch. He had a sleeveless t-shirt on and was sitting at the kitchen table where nine empty bottles of beer were lined up. "I stopped with the hard stuff," he said when he saw me counting. "I want to show you something." He pushed himself up, carrying the bottle he was working on into the bedroom where a big brass-studded trunk was sitting open on the bed. "Take a look," he said.

There was a soldier's uniform folded inside, and I knew it must have been his to wear in Korea. There was a canteen, too, but Bud lifted out something that turned out to be a picture of a group of soldiers when he unrolled it. "You see the lot of us there?" he said. "At the front all of 1952. Me right there on the end—see?"

I saw him standing there in a uniform that looked just like the one in the trunk, and then I noticed that there was a small dot penciled on the chest of the man standing to his left. When I looked at the rest of the picture, I saw dots on a lot of those men. "The dead ones," Bud said like he could read my mind. "That's what the dots are for. You want to know how many? Twenty-six. There's nearly eighty men in that picture. You're going to seventh grade, so I'd bet you could figure what percentage that is. We all stood up for each other. Nobody wanted to die, but nobody wanted to be the man who didn't fight."

He put his beer down on the nightstand beside the bed. I didn't move. I stared at the man standing next to Bud Hutka with a dot on his chest. He was smiling like everybody in my class had when we'd posed for our school picture.

He rolled up the photo and stuffed it back in the trunk. "Just like that?" he said, poking one finger so hard into my chest I had to catch myself against the wall to keep from losing my balance. He picked up his beer and slammed the trunk shut. "Take a look at yourself," he said, turning me toward the mirror. There was a white dot on my chest where he'd poked me. He held me in place until it faded away.

"You see?" Bud said, and when I nodded, he grinned and reached under the bed, sliding a rifle out and carrying it to the window. "Look out there," he said, pointing the rifle barrel like a finger.

It didn't take me long to spot Wayne Cook and his friends standing where they'd been before. "They come back as soon as they think I'm gone," he said, lifting the rifle and aiming it toward the boys. "You see how easy?"

I didn't know what to say except, "Yes."

"They wouldn't look like you do afterwards. They wouldn't look like actors."

"I guess not."

I heard a click as Bud pulled the trigger. "It's not guesswork," he said. "It's a sure thing."

After he pushed the rifle back under the bed, I followed Bud back downstairs. When he walked into the yard, the three boys turned and left. "They're learning," he said before he yanked June up from her chair and guided her inside.

I waited, but June didn't say anything, not even, "What?" The door slammed behind them. I picked up June's half-filled glass and drank what was left. I poured another splash of Four Roses over the ice cubes and drank it straight, feeling its fire slide down my throat. Instead of going directly home, I took a cigarette from June's pack of Pall Malls and walked back to where Wayne and his friends had been standing. The patch of weeds in the vacant lot was trampled, so I knew exactly where they'd been. I looked at the porch, but June didn't come back outside. I sat down and watched for a few minutes, wishing I carried matches so I could light that cigarette. Finally, I put it in my pocket and let myself flop back, limp, my arms and legs flung out to the side, my eyes closing.

"Georgie," I heard. "Georgie."

I opened my eyes and saw June standing in the yard. "You should get up from there," she said, and I sat up so quickly I felt light headed, taking a moment before I pushed myself back up to standing. "It's hard to stop doing something you like, isn't it? I thought you were over that. I thought you were growing up."

* * *

One Sunday morning in early August, my mother turned to look at me and my sister where we sat in the back of the station wagon on the way to church. "There's been a near tragedy," she said, but she didn't look sad. "Two boys from that plan behind us almost got themselves killed."

"How?" I said at once.

"A car crash. Let that be a lesson to you."

I didn't ask what lesson that was, but there were several I knew she wanted me to consider: driving fast, never going to church, drinking.

Paul Kagle, that afternoon, said, "How about that? Wayne Cook's friends, and bad enough to be in the hospital. Cook didn't have a scratch on him, but he's not sixteen yet, so my Dad says he'll have more to worry about than a few broken bones." I wondered if Bud Hutka had sighted on both boys two weeks before or whether he'd chosen Wayne Cook because anyone could tell he was the leader. I wondered if Bud would celebrate the news. It rained all weekend. I didn't see June or Bud. And I felt so strange I didn't play with myself for three days.

The next Saturday afternoon it rained again, but Sunday I saw June Hutka laying out. Johnny Ray was singing "Just Walking in the Rain." There was no sign of Bud. The grass in her yard was high. I thought she needed somebody to cut it; I thought I'd walk up and ask her. Bud had always used a push mower like the one my father owned. It wasn't that noisy, and I'd be able to hear every song she played. "I'll do it for free," I heard myself saying, something that would make her smile in a wistful way that was a prelude to tears.

But without Bud working in the yard on a Sunday, she looked different, and I didn't move from where I stood in my backyard. She lay still the whole time I watched, not sitting up to drink or smoke. Johnny Ray started over again six times, but after a few minutes, it was like looking at a magazine.

After dinner, as it was getting dark, I put on a shirt, took the cigarette and a pack of matches from where I'd hidden them behind my set of Hardy Boys books, walked directly out of our backyard, and cut between two houses to reach the street that ran through the housing plan. I put the cigarette in my mouth and lit it. I wanted to walk in the near darkness to see how it felt looking like somebody else. I didn't try to inhale, but the cigarette glowed when I sucked on it. I could be a hood in the dark. I could be a boy with a pack of Lucky Strikes and a lighter from Atlantic City. My back itched, and I reached up to peel off a curl of skin from my shoulder, but there was nothing there. The cigarette burned down nearly to my lips, and I dropped it on the street and crushed it with my shoe.

There was less than a month left in summer. I walked to where I'd sprawled after drinking the Four Roses, sat down, and decided I'd stay until ten o'clock, which had to be only a few minutes away.

From where I sat I could see all seven houses on our side of the street. Five had lights on, including ours, the kitchen and living room. My sister would be in bed by now. My father would be at the table eating ice cream like he always did before going to bed. My mother would be sitting on the couch working the crossword puzzle from Sunday's paper, trying to get it finished before the answers arrived tomorrow morning. After that, she always said, there was no point because anybody could peek and then pretend they hadn't. In a few minutes, I thought, she'd open the back door and look out, scanning the yards to find me before she called my name.

The house where the Hutkas lived was completely dark. June might have been sleeping at ten o'clock, but with Bud gone for nearly two weeks now, I decided she was out having drinks in some bar with a jukebox that played sad songs like the ones by Johnny Ray. Right then I imagined that if I could stay outside for another hour something a song might be about would happen. And before my mother came to the door, I hunched down and worked my way to the back of the house where the Hutkas' bedroom window was open.

I heard a voice then, like somebody taking a breath after they'd held it as long as they could. And then the sound came again, more than a breath, and I knew it was June Hutka. There was no other voice, June humming now, and I knew this was sex she was enjoying, but by herself, the way I enjoyed it, tuned to what made her moan out loud. I sat against the wall, the window two feet above my head, memorizing the way she sounded, keeping my hands away from my body so I wouldn't scream with her in the dark.

ALL THE BIG THINGS

BECAUSE THE OTHER YOUNG WOMEN the newspaper interviewed were being left behind for the first time, Connie forgave them for saying things like, "I know he'll be careful," and "I'll pray every day for him," as if any of that would make a difference. Her husband Duane had been deployed and finished his tour, but he hadn't come back. This Duane barely spoke. This Duane threatened her with his eyes and fucked her without foreplay as if he'd paid for her. He was nice to the kids, she gave Duane that, but it was the nice of a school-teacher, not a father. He didn't touch them, not even when he let them peck his cheek in what passed for a kiss.

Connie was sure the newspaper had put her in the article because Duane had signed up for a second tour. That made him a hero to some, and she'd known enough, with a week still to go before he left, to say how much she admired his courage, which was true enough, as long as courage was the same as not giving a damn about what happened to yourself. And she didn't say a word about what a relief it was to have him go.

"Afghanistan II, the Sequel—does it feel any different having lived through the first tour?" the reporter had asked her.

Right now five of the eight movies at the mall theaters were sequels—cartoons, comedies, comic book characters. And crime, she thought—as if what was successful was any kind of movie whose subject started with C.

"I can't wait for the movie to end," she said, and he'd smiled as if she'd said something clever. He looked years younger than Duane, who wouldn't be twenty-three until he was two months deep in Afghanistan, but she knew he must have at least graduated from college. My husband, she could have told him, is capable of killing a fool like you.

"They picked me out for my kids," is what she told Duane's mother, Doris. "They made sure I was holding the both of them for the picture."

"There's a danger in that," Doris said. "Now the whole world knows you're by yourself in that house."

"Mom, really."

"All sorts read the papers."

"Not so much anymore, Mom. Now they check Facebook."

"Those people," Doris said, her expression as fixed as a funeral director's. "Those people are just asking for it."

When the article was printed with a sidebar that included pictures of all three soldiers who were being deployed, Connie clipped it and showed it to Duane. The photo of Duane in uniform was the one she'd kept on the kitchen table like a centerpiece during his first tour.

"You saving this?" he said.

"It's something for the girls to have."

"'He's a good soldier,'" Duane read aloud, and the way he made the words sound brought heat to her face. "They're talking bullshit here."

"It doesn't matter what those other women are saying. It's a keepsake for the girls."

Duane crumpled it into a tight ball. "Not anymore," he said, leaving it on the table. And when Clarice, their five-year-old daughter, had tried, a few minutes later, to straighten it, Duane had slapped her hand hard.

Clarice hadn't cried, but her younger sister, Torrie, started bawling. Duane had smoothed out the article then and handed it to Clarice, kissing her forehead before moving to Torrie and doing the same.

"I'll be gone in two days," he said after they ran into the living room. "They can worship that thing all they want after that."

* * *

The day after Duane left, Doris showed up at her door at 8:30 in the morning. "Let's get you and the doll babies out of this house," she said.

"You should have called. What if you drove the twenty-two miles and we weren't here?"

Doris smiled and waved at the girls as they tumbled from their room. "If I'd called, you would've said 'no.' I packed a lunch for everybody for after we look at all the animals I know are just waiting for the girls to enjoy."

"The zoo?" Connie said. "That's more than an hour."

"It's five minutes," Doris said. "Come on, sweethearts. You'll love this."

Two miles outside of town, where the land spread out into farms, Doris parked on the shoulder. "Good as any zoo," she said. A dozen cows stared through the thin wires that Connie knew must be electrified. Clarice and Torrie pressed their faces against the side window.

Connie stared through the windshield and counted. She reached thirty-eight before Clarice said, "We want horses" and Torrie echoed her twice. "That takes money," Doris said, and Torrie, who'd turned three a few days before the newspaper called, began to cry.

"We don't have any money," she wailed.

"Good one, Mom," Connie said.

"The farmers are the ones who need the money, pumpkin," Doris said. "Everything's free for us out here. You keep an eye on those cows for a few more minutes while I get my bearings. You'll see horses soon enough."

"Horses, horses, horses," the girls chanted, but they were looking out the window again.

"There's a place an hour from here where there's a cave you ride through in a boat and they have buffalo there just like these cows inside a fence. You can walk right up to them."

Connie glanced back to see whether her daughters were listening, but they'd become entranced again. "The kids would love it."

"It costs a pretty penny."

"We're not poor, Mom."

"You will be if you fritter it away. Cows are big as buffalo. Just look at the size of them. They're downright ugly, though."

"Cows are cute," Clarice said.

"Cows are cute," Torrie shouted. "Cows are cute."

"My little echo," Doris said. She had the car rolling slowly along the shoulder, keeping all four tires on the packed dirt even though the road stayed empty.

"Bye-bye cows," Torrie shouted, and Connie felt herself holding her breath, afraid that Clarice might echo her sister.

"Seat belts," she said, but the girls seemed transfixed by the bumps that jostled them like an amusement park ride. A few hundred yards hobbled by until two horses appeared near a white wooden fence. "Horses!" Torrie screamed.

"Just like going from one cage to another," Doris said.

"For lions and tigers," Connie said. "What's next? Pigs?"

"This is the farm where that young girl fell off her Daddy's tractor," Doris said. "Fred Salzberg. He bought those two beauties up ahead after the accident. You know."

"The girls don't need to hear that, Mom."

"I'm just saying. You never can tell. She might walk right up to us here with her empty socket and all the rest. Here she is living right among all these animals we come to see. I'll bet she never leaves the farm."

To shut Doris up, Connie opened her door and signaled to the girls, who clambered out. The horses, as if expecting a treat, thrust their heads over the fence, and Connie lifted Torrie up so she could touch the darker one. Her daughter petted it.

After a minute, Connie set Torrie down and reached for Clarice, who said, "No," and backed away. "OK then," Connie said, and lifted Torrie again, holding her while Clarice picked the wild daisies that grew along the fence. Nobody came out of the house during the ten minutes they spent there.

* * *

"That poor girl will never get over it," Doris said, starting right in again after the girls ran off to play at the town playground before it was time for lunch. "Just think about the chances of the tire catching her just so, not crushing her, just tearing her face—it's one of those things nobody can explain. Kids ordinarily get killed on a farm when they fall like that."

Connie watched the girls taking turns on the small slide. "If she gets her face taken care of properly and gets out of her house, she'll be OK. If she moved away, she'd be better off than that."

"You sound just like Duane with that sort of talk. He was always one for wanting to be somewhere that doesn't look like home. You and Duane hit it off thinking like that. Maybe you'll move somewhere when he gets back and leave Mom all by herself here where she's always lived."

"Didn't you ever want to go some place different, Mom?"

"Duane's father was a homebody. I'm talking about you and Duane when you were just showing with Clarice going all the way out West where everything looks like it's in another country."

"It was his graduation present from his grandparents."

"A honeymoon, as it turned out."

"Duane picked all the places—Zion, Bryce, Canyonlands. Everything out there except the Grand Canyon because everybody had seen that."

"Not everybody," Doris said. "Not me. Not Duane's father when he was with us. Not his Uncle Alex and his Aunt Ellen living over to Buffalo on the same street as their parents their whole lives."

"Not me either. Duane made sure we missed it."

"You know what I wished I'd been there to see? Those arches you told me about made right out of those big rocks. How long it must take to hollow out a rock like that. It must take forever."

"Close to it."

"Something like that makes you know those people who believe the world started in the Garden of Eden don't have it right."

"Not if they think it all started 6,000 years ago."

"My Gregory thought that way and never changed his mind."

"It probably gave him comfort when the cancer set in."

"I'm not going to have that to fall back on," Doris said. "I know where I'll be, right there, forever in that hole in the ground."

"Mom."

"You know what? Those cows back there don't know how good they have it. They don't know how ugly they are, and on top of that, they think that farm is all there is and ever will be. You don't see them worrying about all the big things."

* * *

Without Connie asking, the girls made pictures for their daddy. Every day. They pinned them on the bulletin board in their room for a week, and then they took them down and started all over again. Connie stacked and dated the old ones, and she noticed there was always a sun or a full moon in every sky. There were lots of animals, all of them bigger than the people in the pictures. Cows and horses, Connie figured. Maybe sheep and goats. And the willow tree in the front yard was never forgotten if they drew the house, reminding Connie how Duane's father, only months from dying, had tried to talk Duane out of buying the house because of it. "Willows want your water," he'd said. "They'll get after your pipes, and then you'll have mess on your hands."

"That tree was there before the house," Duane had said. As if that settled it.

"Daddy will have a thousand pictures to look at when he gets home," Clarice said. The willow tree looked like it was made of rain in all of her pictures.

"Almost."

"It will take him forever to look at them all."

She thought of Duane with half a 30-pack in a cooler beside him in the living room, watching a *Criminal Minds* Marathon, episodes that started with women and even kids getting murdered. As far as Connie could tell, the only victims who ever lived long enough to be rescued were abducted in the second half of the show. He'd watch three episodes from 8 to 11 and then go for a walk. An hour later he'd come back and go to sleep just after midnight.

For a while she thought there was a decency in his waiting for the girls to go to sleep before he started drinking, but then she would catch him looking at the clock as they finished dinner at 6:30. And he always poured the ice while the girls were awake because they loved watching it tumble from the plastic bag. He'd let them pick a few pieces to suck on after he spread the ice over the cans. "Daddy's picnic," Torrie said, and for a while Connie hoped she might even believe it was the same beer being kept cold until one night, as Torrie crawled into bed, she said, "Daddy drinks every one, doesn't he? He doesn't waste any." So accurate, Connie shuddered, because Duane always finished exactly fifteen and took the empties with him when he left the house. And each afternoon he was home he went to the gym. If habits and discipline were what she wanted in a husband, Duane was perfect, but she knew he had only as many as he needed to avoid talking to her.

* * *

Duane's mother carried the newspaper article in her purse, pulling it out when she visited as if touching the one on the refrigerator was taboo. "'I'm working bargains with God,'" she read one afternoon, quoting what one of the other wives had said. "'I'm making pledges and vows and hoping my good behavior helps to pay for his safety. My pastor tells me faith is comfort, and that's exactly why I agree with him.'"

"Those other women sounded like they believed what they were saying. God and all that."

Doris seemed to be listening, as if she heard God's footsteps on the porch. "You keep that to yourself, young lady. Next thing your babies will hear it."

"You're the one who doesn't expect a thing."

"There's knowing it and then there's saying it. You keep them separate when you have children around."

Connie nodded. It was easy to agree about the knowing and not saying. She kept a lot from Doris, and all of it had to do with Duane. "Without a scratch," Doris had repeated for weeks after Duane came home. "You're so lucky." She still insisted, hoping even after Connie had extended what she called a "grace period" into a third month.

Decompression—Connie had seen that analysis in a dozen articles about returning veterans, but nobody mentioned just how many fathoms somebody might have to ascend through.

Connie stared across the kitchen to where the side door to the garage was closed, the window glass still absent from the night Duane punched it, saying, "Better that than you" the next day, as if he'd done her a favor. "That window's so small," she said. "And yet you never get it taken care of."

"Some day," Connie said. She crossed the kitchen and called Clarice and Torrie for lunch, but Doris wasn't through.

"Everybody knows 'some day' never comes."

"I could cover that whole window with that Bible of Dad's that sits out on your coffee table like some kind of empty flower pot," Connie said. "I can't believe you ever open it, the way you talk."

"It's what's left of Gregory. He wouldn't want it moved. It's his until I die."

The girls ran to the kitchen sink and started pumping the liquid soap dispenser, Torrie scrambling onto a small stool to reach. "For a while there, you'd see that hand soap everywhere," Doris said. "Like people were afraid to touch anything that wasn't wiped down."

"It's called a placebo, Mom. People think they're healthier because they slather their hands with goop."

"You don't believe in soap?" Doris asked. Clarice screamed that the water was too hot, and when she whirled around, soapy water splashed in a small arc onto the floor. Doris frowned. "Somebody will slip and fall, sure as I'm standing here."

"Soap's real. Safety isn't."

"That's not a good attitude with a man in combat in some god-forsaken place."

"He made the call, Mom."

"I can count to a thousand," Torrie said as Connie handed her a paper towel, and without prompting she began, "One two three four . . ."

"What comes after three hundred?" Clarice said.

"Four hundred," Connie said.

Doris shook her head. "You should ask her what comes before it so she learns to count backwards to when your Daddy gets home."

"Two hundred and ninety-nine," Clarice said as she wiped her hands on her shirt.

"Right now today it's three hundred and twenty-two days until your Daddy walks through that door. Did you know that?"

"No."

"Well, now you know. You just keep subtracting. School starts for you in two weeks. When it's over he'll be almost here."

"I want to go to school," Torrie said.

* * *

A week after Duane had broken the window, Connie had suggested a vacation. "Just the two of us," she'd said. "The girls can stay with your Mom." And when he hadn't said, "No," she'd given him a choice of Florida or California, some place warm at the end of April when upstate New York could occasionally suffer a snow squall. He'd opted for a lodge in a rain forest in Washington, and they'd flown to Seattle and settled in for five days of hiking. Ponchos were essential. Everything seemed to be ferns and cedars, the gloom made darker by the intermittent rain and what seemed to be constant cloud cover. Duane was tireless. He led her deep into places where she grew fearful of getting lost. "Look," he said, showing her the occasional sun as if it were a street sign. "Listen," and she had until she heard the sound of water flowing in a creek. "There are so many clues, you can't get lost," he told her, and on the third day, he had her take the lead after they'd walked for hours. "Get us back," he said, but after an hour, he'd taken the lead again.

"There's only one more day before we have to go home," she said the next morning.

"Yeah," Duane had said, but the tone made it sound as if he'd said "good."

On the plane he told her he'd re-upped. "As if you're asking for it," she'd said, and his expression hadn't changed. As if he knew the truth of what she said, or as if he thought she was wrong but it didn't matter enough to argue.

* * *

In the grocery store with Doris, a week before Clarice would begin first grade, Connie spotted the girl who'd lost an eye. Her hair hung across her scars like cloth, but Connie could make out the stitched shut, empty socket. "Let's go pick out cereal," she said to Clarice and Torrie, but they'd already noticed the girl.

Neither girl spoke, but they stood still and stared. The one-eyed girl followed her father, who hunched his shoulders as if dragging her into an adjoining aisle. Connie remembered what the father had said in the newspaper: "My Harvester had flushed birds and turned over two nests of mice before I let her crouch behind me, hugging my neck, in shorts and t-shirt. Her thin little legs were still white because it was so early in May."

"What's wrong with that girl?" Clarice said. Connie was thankful Torrie didn't echo her for once.

"She was a little girl who was riding on a tractor with her Daddy when she tumbled off and got run over."

"She should get an eye patch like a pirate," Clarice said. "Or a pretend eye."

"She has to wait until she's all done growing," Connie said. She didn't know if that was true, but she hoped there was a reason besides not having enough money. Holding hands, the girls ran ahead, looking down each aisle, but they didn't act as if they'd spotted the one-eyed girl and her father.

"Can you imagine ruining your own child that way?" Doris whispered right into Connie's ear. Connie could. She thought about it constantly—her children hit by cars, mauled by dogs, poisoned by cleanser or insect repellent. So close to that unfortunate girl, Connie believed that her daughters' tragedies had merely been postponed.

"You know what I'd worry about if I were you?" Doris said. "Duane comes home crippled some way on his face—cut up all to hell, or burned real bad, you know. Scars. Something people look at and then they can't tell who he was before all that. I have to admit I'd rather have him dead so people remember who he was when he was all in one piece."

Connie pushed her shopping cart in front of the aisle lined on one side by cereal boxes. "Get the girls back here," she said. "We need to do what we came here for."

An hour later, with Doris in the house promising to make spaghetti, Connie took a walk by herself, choosing to cut between the houses across the street before setting off along a side road that led out of town. She caught herself hurrying nearly into a trot and made herself slow down. She felt like a ghost who had to leave her house before she entered her body.

Ten minutes later, she came to a stretch of cornfields that ended in what looked to be acres of plowed land she couldn't imagine being planted this late in the summer. A farm this close to town seemed strange, but she'd walked here before. There'd been a For Sale sign posted when she and Duane had moved in two years ago. One early morning, when Duane had still been home, she'd passed a tractor idling in the driveway to the barn. A red John Deere. The farmer had been crouched beside it as if he were speaking to it.

His last morning home, packed and ready for another year away, Duane had pulled a smile down over his face like a sweater, but it felt so insincere the girls hesitated when he called them. They cried and looked at Connie, who said, "Give Daddy a goodbye hug and kiss."

And when it was her turn, she recognized his expression as the one she'd seen as their trip to the rainforest had wound down. It was the smile of a graduate, a combination of relief and joy.

* * *

"I need to take a look at this," Doris said after they'd finished the spaghetti and the girls were busy making another drawing. She tugged the newspaper article off the refrigerator and examined it as if the feature might have been revised.

"Where's that copy you keep?"

"It creased so much it tore. I taped it and laid it out on my dresser so I don't have to handle it."

Connie watched as Doris folded the article in half. "You can read it without taking it off the fridge."

"No, I can't. I have to have it just so."

"Where's that?"

"I know how it should look when I can read it comfortable."

Connie glanced at the photos of herself and the other young women. She remembered that one woman claimed the photo of herself was off-center on purpose. "I'm saving that space like a good seat at a sold-out show," the woman had said. "He's running late. That's what I tell myself."

"I want you to have a place," Duane had said when they'd bought the house. "Just in case" is what he didn't say. She could have mentioned that when the reporter talked to her, Connie thought. She could have set up a scene like that woman she'd never meet again.

"Listen," Doris said, "after the girls are tucked in, I have a surprise for you. Wait till you see what I brought." Connie nodded, but she kept her eyes on the newspaper article as Doris unfolded it and stuck it under the magnets.

"Here we are," Doris said two hours later. She skidded a fat plastic tub across the carpet with her foot and settled down beside it. "Pictures," she said. "There's so many here you'll have to fall in love with some of them."

Connie saw that the tub was nearly full of slides. Thousands, all of them loose. Rather than sit on the floor, she sat on the couch, but Doris was already busy. "Duane had the biggest smile all the way back there in grade school before you two knew you were on the same planet. His daddy kept taking pictures that were slides way after nobody did that. Duane could only find the one place that developed them for him near the end."

Doris lifted a handful of slides and let them drop through her fingers. "Look at all these. Gregory had them all in little packets, but after he died I tossed them into this plastic tub to save space. It's going to take some sorting."

"There's so many."

"You can hold them up to the light and make out what's on them."

"There's a projector somewhere in my house, and we can show your girls whatever pictures you want once we find them."

Connie held up a slide and squinted at what looked like a close up of a rose. Doris reached over and took the slide. "Gregory loved his flowers. Just set those aside."

She looked at six slides before she found one with people, but they were too small to identify. "Who's this?" she said, handing it to Doris.

"Nobody. He was taking a shot of Mt. Vernon and those people were visiting too." When the next slide showed the rhododendron bush in bloom outside Duane's old bedroom window, she sat back and sighed. "I'll check on the girls," she said. "This might take forever."

"You give up too easy."

"There's so many."

"I know Duane's in here a hundred times. From the church picnics, for sure. He was always around. From when he was in the Little League. From Easter when he'd be dressed like a little gentleman."

The girls were sleeping soundly. She watched them for a few minutes, but they didn't show any signs of restlessness. She went to the kitchen and made coffee, taking a few more minutes to get the hang of the coffee maker Doris had brought over the week before, declaring that she was switching to instant because it was less fuss. By the time she returned with two cups, Connie saw three small stacks of slides set aside from a puddle of hundreds.

"Sixteen enough for you?"

"Sure."

"Have yourself a look-see then."

The first showed a crowd of kids from a distance. "Trust me. That one has Duane in it some place." When Connie held up the second one, moving it back and forth as if she could enlarge it by swinging it through the air, Doris said, "That one, too. Gregory must have been expecting something to happen."

In the third one, though, she could pick out Duane as a boy. "You can't complain about that one," Doris said.

"It's nice, Mom. Thank you."

"Maybe the second tour will change him back," Doris said.

"What?"

"I'm not an idiot. He wasn't himself when he was home from all that." She held up another slide. "See him there? Such a good boy. You know what I'm thinking? It was like Duane had fallen off a tractor and had his face pulled off."

* * *

The day before school began, Connie was having a tea party with Clarice and Torrie under the willow when she saw the cow approaching. She thought of the red John Deere on the closest farm, but even from there, the cow would have to manage a half mile of front yards and back yards before trotting to their house at #1, the corner lot. Yet here it was—Connie wanted to say thundering, but that would be a lie—loping to a stop right in front of where she and the girls were holding plastic cups under their willow.

It was a young cow. Not a calf, but not full grown. It snorted and stared at them, the sides of its white-spotted black body heaving. Torrie said "cow" and pointed. There wasn't a soul in sight—no neighbors gawking, no farmer chasing after and hollering out "Bossie" or "Patches" at this half-grown cow that suddenly bellowed out a sound so long and mournful that Clarice crawled to Connie, spilling her teacup, and began to wail, while Torrie looped her arms around Connie's neck in a silent choke hold.

The cow didn't leave as Connie hoped it might. It seemed unwilling to go into the street to the left or straight ahead beyond the willow. The back yard was fenced in, so there was nowhere to go that would keep it on grass except back where it came from. With a huff like the air was let out of it, it settled on the lawn.

There was a string of more than twenty yards along their side of the street, but their yard was the only one with a tree of any size. The rest held dogwoods and weeping cherries and the like, a lot of evergreen bushes shaped into balls or cones or just trimmed flat like a military hair cut. Maybe, Connie thought suddenly afraid, that cow was looking for shade large enough for it to fit inside. It stood again and nosed under the tree, the girls going mute and clutching her.

"Daddy," Clarice whispered.

"Daddy," Torrie said aloud. "Daddy."

The cow nuzzled against Connie. It licked her face. Clarice and Torrie, seeing that big slurping tongue, stopped calling for their father. Torrie reached out her hand and touched the cow's nose, saying, "Wet," and letting go of Connie's neck. Clarice silently touched the cow's face, feeling the texture of its skin.

For nearly a minute, the cow stood still and let them touch it. When it turned away, its tail switching behind it, slapping against the drooping branches, both girls said "Mommy" at the same time, and they watched the cow amble away, beginning to gather speed as it crossed lawns, until it became a speck twenty yards away. They stared, even though, by now, it was so small it could have been anything at all.

PRIVATE THINGS

IN THE CAR ON THURSDAY MORNING, Corey's mother looked directly at him the way she always did when she was driving and said, "Wait until you see where we're going."

Corey didn't answer. If the car didn't break down or crash, he would see whatever his mother had planned. Since his eleventh birthday, he'd entered what his mother called his "silent phase," and he was happy she didn't press him to talk unless, she reminded him, "There's an emergency."

A year ago Corey's mother had decided to homeschool him. "You hate going there anyway," she said, and he'd agreed. Fifth grade was terrible. He was in the middle school now with boys up to eighth grade who said "fuck" and "cocksucker" in the halls between classes, and girls who laughed when they heard those words.

His father, "who wears the religion in this family," according to his mother, didn't approve. "Adversity and temptation are God's fitness training for us," he said. "It's how we grow strong enough to be his soldiers."

"You listen to your father," his mother said, "but never you mind the Jesus talk when you're with me. You'll be the only student, but this is a public school I'm running."

Now, as she parked the car on a street in Philadelphia, she said, "Once we're inside, you have to answer when I talk to you. We'll be in school then." Corey nodded. He liked being in school fifty miles from where they lived near Allentown. And he had signed a contract to do what she asked. "Just you wait," she said. "I've been reading about this place."

It didn't take Corey long to agree with her. Right away they walked into a room with nothing but glass cases full of skulls. They gazed at old photographs of men and women with missing limbs and examined a single prosthetic leg with an inscription that declared it had only been worn once to the owner's daughter's wedding. "Imagine that, Corey," his mother said. "Doesn't that say something about love?"

In another room, Corey saw a photograph of a naked girl with no legs. She was balanced on her hands for the photo, and there were little, worm-like flaps of skin where her hips should have started. He figured his legs must have looked like that a few weeks after he was conceived, right before they unfolded and grew where they were supposed to be instead of curled like a cheap noisemaker for New Year's Eve. His mother nudged him away from the display. "Someone had the good sense to collect all these things, the good with the bad, but we're not here to look at the monsters," she said. "This is school, not the circus." Corey knew there was a woman with a horn growing out of her forehead because her picture was on the free brochure at the entrance, but he didn't complain because his mother allowed him to stop by a set of skeletons.

There was a huge one of someone who'd grown to be seven foot six and was still growing when he died. The sign by the door read *Bone Pathology*, so it wasn't a surprise to see a short skeleton nearby. *Mary Ashberry*, the inscription said, *3'6"*. Little, all right, but what was astonishing was that she held the skull of her child, who, the sign said, had died at birth shortly before Mary Ashberry died from peritonitis after a cesarean section.

"People are often very tall and very short," his mother said. "These aren't the same as those others."

Corey nodded, but the other skeletons looked deformed, the backbones impossibly curved, the shoulders tilted in a way he'd never seen.

"Isn't this the strangest place you've ever been?" she said a half hour later.

"Maybe."

"What do you mean maybe?" She pointed at the nearest display. "What's weirder than a jar full of needles and pins that all came from inside somebody who ate them and still lived?"

Corey thought of the wig his mother had begun wearing at the beginning of the week. "I'm so tired of wasting time with my hair," she'd said when he'd stared.

"It's way more hair than you have," he'd said.

"Good," she'd said, but now he thought for a few more seconds and said, "Church."

"There's something to that, I'll admit," she said, "but don't you let your father hear you say it."

"Sure," he said. It was an easy promise to keep. He talked even less to his father.

"We went to a museum" was all that Corey told his father when they got home. He knew better than to say anything about the kind of museum. Let his father assume he'd looked at dinosaur bones and mummies and old statues. His father believed they wasted a lot of time on things other than the basics, but he mostly hated home-schooling because he thought it was making Corey a sissy. "The world's out there rough and ready," he'd say about once a month. "You don't get any calluses reading books at home."

And when his mother would answer by saying something like, "We don't live on the frontier, Donald," he'd point out whichever window was closest and answer, "That's what you think."

The argument never changed, but Corey was happy to stay home where his mother allowed him to look up all the answers to the tests she gave him. At the middle school, it would be called cheating, but his mother called it an open-book test. She watched television while he took them. Sometimes she went grocery shopping.

* * *

When his father made Corey go to church and be an acolyte, his mother had only said, "Just not Sunday School. Nothing organized like that."

"OK, Mellie. It's a deal," his father had said, but after he left the kitchen, his mother smiled.

"There's more to learn there than your father thinks. You just keep your eyes open and your brain sharp."

Church turned out to be boring, but Corey loved lighting and snuffing the candles. Bowing before he began, bowing after he'd lit the two on the altar, then lighting seven each from bottom to top on the gold-plated candelabras that stood on either side of the altar. One by one they would flare into light, sixteen in all before he bowed once more and pulled the wick inside the candle lighter to extinguish it.

Corey said nothing to his parents, but he liked wearing the surplice, like the people in the choir did. And he liked to watch as the church organist helped the minister fill tiny glasses set in trays with wine on communion Sundays. It took them nearly twenty minutes to fill a dozen trays, and Corey carried them to the altar a half hour before church began, taking a minute to stand at the pulpit while all the pews were empty. It was as if he knew secrets. Like the people who made television happen must feel when they saw how people acted before the cameras came on. But the only other thing Corey liked about church was watching his father collect the offering in his dark suit and tally up the contributions every Sunday. He helped pass around the plates where people laid envelopes marked to show how much was inside and how they wanted it to be used—Current or Benevolent or Building Fund—to pay the church's bills, help some charity, or prepare for an addition to the church.

Corey's father had told him there were people who gave only to one of the three, how some felt charity was the church's work or bill-paying was the only reason to give. But when the plate went by Corey, he noticed that there were people who just dropped money in without an envelope.

"Naked," his father said. "There's those who think it's nobody's business what they give, not even if it helps to have a statement at tax time. And some are big givers. You'd be surprised."

Corey knew his family received a statement four times a year. "Your father gives too much," his mother said. "That's all I'm saying about that."

"I tithe. That's what God expects," Corey's father said. "It's like tipping. You give 10 percent for good service."

His mother chuckled. "Not where I come from."

* * *

"We're going to town today," Corey's mother said the following Thursday. "We'll study shopping."

Corey knew he'd made a face when she blocked the front door as he walked across the kitchen. "Going shopping is part of school," she said. "Your father's always moaning about how you're not learning to get along in the world, so let's do some fundamentals. What does his public school do except allow every Tom, Dick, and Harry inside?"

"So why not the mall?" he said.

"Town is different. It's where people own the places where they work. You need to see this before it's in a museum, too."

They started at a clothing store for women. "I'll buy here," she said. "You watch now so you understand how it works."

A half hour went by before his mother laid out a dress on the counter by the register and ran her fingers along the seams. Corey saw how the clerk glanced at his mother's wig because it must have been bumped off center in the dressing room. "Look there," his mother said. "See how the stitching isn't tight. I'll be sewing this before too long."

The clerk nodded. She looked as if she were still in high school. She was wearing a black sweater with a red dragon swirling up across her breasts. It didn't look like anything that was on display in the store. "We don't sew them," she said. "It's not our fault."

"But you could make up for it," his mother said. "There are ways to make it right. Move it to the sale rack where customers know problems come with their purchases."

"We don't sell seconds here."

"I know how these things work," his mother said. "I stood in your shoes for years. It's a hard thing having to follow store policy when you know what's right. And here I am just falling in love with this dress almost enough to overlook the stitching."

As soon as the clerk hesitated, Corey knew his mother had taught him something. The girl explained how she wasn't authorized to mark down merchandise, how she had to consult the owner. His mother smiled and thanked her for taking the trouble. They waited while the girl entered a back room, and when she reappeared, she offered 15 percent off.

"You have to Jew these people down," his mother said after they left. "It's what they expect. Shopkeepers. Repairmen. Your father is a pharmacist where everybody pays list price, but these people are used to it. And just think how much they make on that dress from those who don't know any better."

Corey looked in the window of each store. His mother seemed to have forgotten about the end of independent businesses. Or maybe, he thought, it was supposed to be self-explanatory because half of the stores were closed, their display windows empty. Like skeletons, he thought, until he noticed one with a full display of houses and businesses for sale, all of the advertisements yellowed. His mother had already stopped. "Look at those prices," she said. "They sound like bargains now." He read the numbers on three of the ads while his mother used the window's reflection to adjust her wig.

During the afternoon, they watched Jerry Springer interview three fat women who said they were cheating on their marriage with their husbands' brothers. He and his mother ate potato chips from a bag large enough to be called *The Weekender*. It usually lasted two afternoons, and then his mother would say they were fasting until a week went by and they devoured a new bag. "This is recess," she said as the brothers came from behind the curtain to confront the married couples. "Just listen to these people and you'll know why I'm teaching you. You can bet they all went to the public school."

* * *

Sunday morning Corey's father turned off the road half way to church and drove slowly along streets lined with double houses.

"She doesn't have a car, this woman who comes into the drugstore for prescriptions," he said. "The kind you rely upon. And she has a boy your age. You probably didn't notice, but she started attending six weeks ago."

The boy's name was Frank, he had the shadow of a mustache, and Corey didn't think he looked anything like twelve. He was happy when Frank didn't say a word in the car or when he sat beside him in the pew. He watched one of the other two boys who were acolytes put out the candles and followed his father into a room behind the chancel where he tallied up the offering. "She had a ride home," his father said. "She knows I have business back here for an hour. You and Frank hit it off?"

"I don't know," Corey said, but he was already opening envelopes for his father to hurry things along. The church had around four hundred people attend each week, a lot of envelopes and plenty of loose dollars in the plate.

Corey handed his father the bills and the checks that were inside after he made sure they were for the same amount as the numbers printed on the outside. His father had told him it was OK for him to know the names because he didn't know these people and he didn't go to school with their children. Marvin Childress gave five dollars each week. Simon Donnelly gave seventy-five. Only two people gave more than his father.

His father always counted the loose offering by himself, but Corey could see there were stacks of fives and tens and twenties before his father handed him $1.50 for the soda machine in the church's basement rec room. He would drink a root beer and wonder why Marvin Childress would let the church know how cheap he was when some people dropped twenty dollars or more into the plate without asking for a receipt.

When they walked into the house, Corey's mother was lying

under a blanket on the couch as if she'd been taking a nap. "So how was church?" she said.

"Different," Corey said.

His mother sat up, and he could see she was still in her pajamas even though she was wearing her wig. "How's that?" she said.

"We sat with a boy and his mother."

"Who?"

"We gave them a ride from Cherry City. The boy didn't talk. Just Dad talked, and the woman sometimes answered."

"You're quite the storyteller today," she said.

"For charity's sake, Mellie," his father said. "She's a cleaning woman without a car. She comes in for prescriptions. Necessary ones."

"A woman who housecleans. Those pills must cost her a fortune. Is her boy an acolyte, too?" She was standing now, holding the blanket around her body with both hands.

"He's the same age as Corey, or at least thereabouts. They moved here two months ago. The boy doesn't know anybody, and here it is the school year starting."

"Maybe we'll visit them," his mother said. "For school."

"You do that, Mellie. Give him a test while you're at it."

"He'd have to come to the pharmacy for some of the answers, Donald. Should I send him?"

His father glanced at the living room window as if he was about to point out the frontier. "If you came to church, you'd understand, Mellie."

"Yes, I would. You can count on that."

* * *

The next morning his mother drove Corey toward the street where Frank and his mother had been waiting on the corner.

"Somewhere around here," he said, and she parked.

"Your father knows I'd never leave you on a street like this," she said. "Anything could be going on here. Anything at all."

"You're right," Corey said, and his mother looked at him.

"He speaks," she said, but she was already striding toward the end of the block. "Look at this place closely," his mother said, and they turned and walked and turned again until Corey was unsure how to get back to where she'd parked the car. When they made another turn and crossed through an alley, she pivoted quickly onto another street and Corey felt lost. Without speaking, he kept walking as if they were in the mall. He thought the neighborhood couldn't be so big he could really become confused.

"You didn't even check the name of the street, did you?"

"No."

"Where do you think you are?"

Where the boys who say "fuck" and "cocksucker" live, he wanted to say. There were toys scattered on sidewalks, discarded appliances on porches. Corey saw a full set of bald tires in one yard. A few had flower beds—"Those people there are trying," his mother said. "What do you imagine they think about their neighbors?

"And just you remember the boys who live here go to the middle school. We're five miles from our house, but this is still part of the district." She crossed the street and slowed down. "I'm tired," she said. "Let's go home and watch Springer. Maybe he'll have somebody from this neighborhood on today."

* * *

"Last night your mother said she took you to Cherry City," his father said on the way to church the next Sunday. "She waited a good long time to let me know."

"We just walked around. We didn't have to go inside to know what it was like there."

"That's your mother talking," his father said. "She can be wrong, you know."

"I know."

"Do you now?" When they didn't turn toward Cherry City, Corey wondered what else his mother had said the night before. His father kept his eyes forward. "Your mother doesn't work," he said. "She thinks she's a teacher, but she doesn't get paid, so what does that make her?"

"I learn something every day."

"You'd better, because you're missing something every day, too." Corey watched how his father's hands were tight around the steering wheel as if it took muscle to turn it. His mother had let Corey drive a few times in the parking lot at the nearby Catholic Church. He knew how easily the wheel turned. "Your mother won't say it," his father went on, "but she hates people. That's what makes her the way she is."

"What way is that?" Corey said.

"You don't need me to tell you."

Corey shook his head, but he knew what his father meant. His mother did everything herself because she didn't think anybody could do anything right. But she was the one who'd grown up in a place like Cherry City. His father's parents belonged to a country club.

***

Frank and his mother were standing on the sidewalk by the front door when Corey and his father arrived. Frank was wearing the same open-collar, black shirt with jagged white Chinese symbols above the pockets that he'd worn the week before. "Why don't you and Frank sit together where you want to today?" his father said. "I know you don't want to be sitting beside us like you're in grade school."

His father followed Frank's mother into the pew they'd occupied the week before. "It's your church," Frank said. "Where's a place that isn't gay?"

"The balcony."

Frank glanced toward the stairs to their left. "Less gay, at least," he said, and then he looked Corey up and down. "You look like you're going to prom."

Corey imagined asking Frank if he knew how to read his shirt. "I don't mind," he said.

"You're the only boy wearing a tie. What do you wear to school?"

"Whatever I want." Which was true.

"I bet."

During the service Frank drew pictures on his bulletin. An eagle. A skeleton. "Not bad," Corey printed on his bulletin so Frank could see what he'd written.

Frank pulled the bulletin out of Corey's hands and began to draw. When he passed it back, there was a picture of a penis inside a pair of lips. "Church sucks," it said underneath it. Corey reminded himself not to forget to throw the bulletin in the trash before he met his father to count the offering.

"Why do you come all the way down here for church?" he asked Frank while his father talked to Frank's mother after the service ended.

"My old lady drags me here. If I don't come with her, I don't get an allowance."

"She pays you to come to church?"

"Yeah, I guess. She says it's worth it. But look around. You see anybody else our age except girls? Even you. You're not my age. I'm in eighth grade, and I bet you're in seventh or even sixth."

Corey saw his father wave them toward the receiving line. "I'm twelve."

"What? You don't want to tell me what grade you're in? You get held back or something?"

"I don't go to your school."

"Lucky you," Frank said, and he turned his back, getting ahead of Corey into the line with his mother, who hurried him through with a quick handshake.

"So," the minister said to Corey, "are you the Good Samaritan?"

The tone of the minister's voice made Corey believe, for a moment, that this was a test. "I'm not sure," he said.

"God bless," the minister answered, as if he hadn't heard. It sounded like the end of a sermon, the part where the minister lifted his hands and bowed his head simultaneously, beginning a short prayer that preceded the collection of the offering.

"Thank you," his father said, laying a hand on Corey's shoulder as if he'd grown younger during church, but the minister was already extending his hand toward an old woman who was next in line.

When he began opening envelopes two minutes later, Corey opened three of them slowly, then asked to be excused. He still had the bulletin in his pocket, and he needed to find a trash can where somebody besides him and his father might toss something. When he returned, his father looked impatient. "What's the matter?" he said.

"Nothing."

"Sure there is."

Corey thought about how deeply he'd pushed the bulletin into the can that stood just inside the main door of the church. Frank was right about how few boys there were in church. He needed the janitor to dump that can without paying any attention to what was in it. "Is Frank's mom like Frank?" he said.

His father rested one finger on the column of figures he had in front of him before he answered. "What's that supposed to mean?"

"You know."

"Your mother is sick. I'm sure you know that by now."

"How sick?" Corey said, though he'd known all along what that wig meant.

"That's not for me to say. But it's not the flu we're talking about."

Corey thought it was breast cancer or ovarian cancer, some secret part of his mother gone wrong. His father was embarrassed by ads for tampons. But if his mother wouldn't say anything, he couldn't ask.

"Frank's mother is like herself, if you really want to know."

"OK," Corey said, but the next morning, after his father left for work, he asked his mother if she knew what sort of prescriptions Frank's mother relied on.

"Those prescriptions mean she's on borrowed time. Is that enough for you to know?"

"She doesn't look sick."

"Maybe she puts on a show for church." She was lying. Corey was sure of it, but he didn't interrupt. "There are people who live for years with problems," she went on. "You know. Like some of those we saw at the museum." She sounded like his father now, though Corey thought it must be terrible for her to say what she didn't believe out of love for him.

"Look here," she said. "I bought you this book about the sorts of things at the museum." Corey stared at the cover, a picture of a small skeleton with an enormous skull split open at the top. "That boy had something called water on the brain," she said. "The poor thing's head eventually opened like a flower." She pushed the book toward him until he laid his hands on it. "You research that now. I'm taking a nap."

Corey looked up water on the brain and discovered the real word was *hydrocephaly*, and it was spinal fluid, not water that seeped between the skull and the brain, the skull pushed out and out until it turned so thin it collapsed. The book had dozens of incredible pictures like the one on the cover. He let his mother sleep.

* * *

The next Sunday was Corey's turn to be acolyte. Wearing his black shirt, Frank sat with him in the front row. He didn't have a bulletin, but Frank didn't draw anything on his, and by the time Corey changed, Frank was gone.

He was sure Frank would make fun of him the following week, maybe draw a picture of a boy in a surplice with a penis in his mouth, but all Frank said was, "Where did you go after the candles were out? Like a backstage kind of place?"

"Yeah," Corey said. "It's pretty cool. You want to see it quick before the service starts?"

"It's part of the church. It can't be that cool." Frank picked up a bulletin and started toward the balcony.

"There's all these bottles of wine back there. For communion. You know. It's like a liquor store."

"Yeah? That's a little bit cool."

"Come on," Corey said. "We only have a few minutes."

Corey was surprised that the cabinet where the wine was kept wasn't locked. Frank reached inside and took out a half-filled bottle. "You ever tasted this?" he said.

"The pastor would know," Corey said, and Frank sneered.

"Check this out. You never drank any of this wine with all of the chances you've had? It's so gay in that blouse thing they make you wear you should get something for doing it." He lifted one of the empty trays from another shelf. "Look at all these tiny glasses. You'd have to drink a whole tray full to feel anything." Corey kept his eye on the tray, afraid Frank would dump the glasses on the carpet. Through the speaker that hung from one wall came the sound of the congregation singing the processional hymn. Frank unscrewed the cap and drank from the bottle. "Here's to communion," he said. "Thank you, Jesus." He drank again and offered the bottle to Corey, who shook his head. "You ought to be the acolyte every week," Frank said. "You're gay enough for it."

"It belongs to the church," Corey said.

Frank grinned. "You don't know what you're missing."

Corey heard the minister begin to lead the congregation through the pledges and creeds that led to the reading of the gospel. "I'll live," he said.

"I know all about your Mommy teaching you. You should go to a real school. All you get at home is the part that sucks."

Corey felt the words, "I'll live" form again, but he smothered them with a shrug, and Frank started back in as if he'd answered. "You don't get to see all the hot girls. All day long they're right in front of you. And field trips. We got a whole day off last week to do nothing but go to the place where they show stars and shit on the ceiling."

"A planetarium."

"Yeah. What, you think I don't know the name because it's a big word? Terrarium. Aquarium. Planetarium. See? And just when it was getting boring, there was music and lasers and shit."

"I've seen that a few times."

"Yeah. At the planetarium, right? Good for fucking you." He took another sip and screwed the cap back on.

Corey heard the anthem end and the sermon begin. "You can't go back now," Frank said. "Communion doesn't happen every week. By the time it comes around again, nobody will remember how full this bottle was."

"Somebody will."

"Somebody like your old man? He's so clueless. He slips me money to put in that bowl. Fuck—like my old lady's too poor to let me give money away."

"Really?"

Frank unscrewed the cap and screwed it back on. "You didn't know? Fuck. I only put the dollar in because I thought you were checking up on me for him."

Corey looked up at the speaker as if he expected to see the minister's mouth forming the words of the sermon. Frank took another sip of the wine, but he seemed to be finished talking. When the recessional hymn began, the bottle put away but Frank looking bleary-eyed beside the closed cabinet, Corey opened the door and walked down the hall the opposite way he'd led Frank to the changing room. When he reached the back steps, he was glad to see that Frank hadn't come out yet. Now he could walk underneath the sanctuary and be standing inside the front door by himself when his father came out.

He made it with half a verse to spare, but his father didn't walk out with Frank's mother. "He was called out during the service," she said. "He wanted you to know it wasn't about your mother."

"OK," Corey said, but her eyes went past him to where Frank was feeling his way up the center aisle, walking as if the floor had turned to slush. Three women filled the aisle behind him, each holding a bulletin over their mouths as they leaned toward each other to talk.

When Frank let go of the last pew, Corey heard Frank's mother say, "Excuse me," before she took two steps forward and hit Frank in the face three times, swinging her open hand left, right and then left again. "God—damn—you," she said in rhythm, and she looked at Corey. "You look sober," she said. "What are you, some kind of voyager for watching badness?"

Frank reddened, and Corey thought he was embarrassed, not because his mother had hit him in front of Corey, but because his mother didn't know the first thing about big words. She grabbed his hand and dragged him out onto the sidewalk. "Where would he get it?" Corey heard one of the three women say. He made his way to the room next to the one he changed in, but it was empty. No envelopes. No loose change. No sign of his father.

He walked to where the car was parked two blocks from the church and waited twenty minutes before his father appeared. His father looked so serious that Corey said, "I sat in the balcony," before he could be asked. "With Frank."

"Is that right?"

It wasn't exactly a lie. The room with the wine was a level up, like the counting room and the balcony. "The sermon was all about the need for tolerance. The pastor told the story about Zaccheus, the tax collector, sitting up in the tree to see Jesus."

Corey's father seemed to soften. "OK," he said, "but you need to get in the car now."

"What about the books?

"Never mind the books. They'll be taken care of."

* * *

Corey's father stayed home from work on Monday; his mother sat in the kitchen without her wig. "I'm not dying," she said. "At least that's what they tell me."

"But your hair's gone."

"Almost," she said. "There's still a few strands that won't let go." She reached across the table and laid her hand over Corey's, and he was surprised how warm it felt.

"I've got a good cancer. Pay attention and look close at my head. This is still school."

She handed him a book with a page dog-eared where it listed all the kinds of cancer according to life expectancies. "Look where it says *thyroid* and tell me what you see."

"Five years: 96%. Ten years: 96%. Twenty years: 95%."

"Twenty years," she said. "I'll be seventy-two by then and have a better chance of dying from a heart attack than this. I'll be past the threescore and ten your father's always citing now that he's past fifty, too. I don't even have a thyroid anymore. They took it out in the summer while you were at camp. That's how easy it was—in and out of the hospital while you were taking swimming lessons and doing crafts."

Corey followed the numbers down past stomach and lung and esophagus to the very last kind: Pancreas—Five years: 4%.

"I know what you're looking at," she said. "Just hope they don't tell you it's in your pancreas when you get cancer someday."

He shut the book so quickly his mother re-opened it. "You don't catch anything by reading about it," she said. "This isn't church."

"OK."

"I'm taking you along to the oncology center in an hour. You take your notebook. This is something you need to know, that's for sure. Now you take a look at what I had to say about your water-on-the-brain essay."

She'd written comments in both margins of all four pages. She'd put a big exclamation point beside where he'd written, "Heads like aliens have, the ones with brains bigger than ours," on page two.

"When I was a girl," she said, "the aliens wanted to kill us all or take over our brains. Now all they do is glow in the dark and look at us like we're patients."

"They're not all like that."

"The ones we remember are. They don't bother to talk anymore. Not even a roar. And they're so skinny and small and sorrowful. It makes me think we're not even worth a good, old-fashioned death ray."

"Mom," Corey started, but she shook her head the way she did when his father jingled his keys in his pocket while she straightened his tie before he left for church. If his mother died, or even if she grew too weak to teach him, Corey knew his father would send him back to the public school where, when he first entered middle school, six neighborhood schools joining into one large building, a group of boys had circled him and asked him where he was from. "Melody Lane," he'd said.

"Before that."

"I've always lived there."

The boys had laughed. One of them had pushed him just before two Down syndrome girls walked by. "Retards," the boy had said, turning back toward his friends. "They're always walking around here like they belong." Public school was like Springer. You could say anything you wanted.

"Your father got himself into a pickle at church," his mother said.

"What?"

"He's been stealing." Two secrets in one morning, Corey thought, and he'd known both of them before he'd been told. "He's been helping himself to the same amount of money he puts in each week."

"That's not stealing."

"That's not how it's being seen."

"Why didn't he just not put anything in the offering?"

"He's always given. He used to give for real."

Corey pictured his father deciding how many twenties, tens, and fives would make up the stash he shoved into the pocket of his black suit coat, changing the mix each week while Corey drank root beer in the church basement. "It's over a hundred dollars a week. I open the envelopes."

"Yes, it is."

"So he could just stay home and not steal and have the same amount of money?"

"That's what he says. We have to believe him. He's waiting to talk with you in the living room."

Corey didn't sit down. He stood in front of the blank television and waited until his father sighed and said, "OK, here's the story: You know what I told you about tipping God. You don't get good service, you withhold."

"So you started when Mom got sick?"

"A little before that. There were other things that went wrong. It's not just about your mother's health."

"Things?"

"Yes. A few."

"Like what?"

"Private things."

Corey wanted to walk away from his father before his father made an excuse that would sound like the ones people who were arrested made. "He drove me to it," or "I couldn't take it any more." As if nobody could admit they were wrong, even though they were.

If his father told him he was a liar, he could admit it, but that was another thing people did, not saying things straight out, just changing their tone or the way they looked at you, making their own lies in return. "Then you haven't given anything for a long time?" Corey said. "You've stiffed God for years?"

He heard his father suck in air as if he were about to go underwater. "You don't always end up doing what you expect to," his father said. "I was going to stop when your mother got better. Definitely."

Corey knew the big word for stealing over and over—kleptomania—but it didn't seem like the appropriate word for stealing from God. He thought of his weekly dollar in the offering plate and the dollar his father had given Frank each week so he could sit beside his mother and believe he was helping her. Right then he hoped his mother was right, that there wasn't a God, because stealing from him would just about guarantee an eternity in hell.

"Nobody's getting arrested," his mother said a minute later. Though she wasn't eating or reading the paper, she'd sat back down at the kitchen table. "But he's finished there, you can be sure of that. We should be thankful it's a minister holding the gun to his head or we'd really be in for it." She pushed her chair back, but she didn't stand. "Your father won't be taking you to church anymore. Do you still want to go?"

"Not there," Corey said at once.

"Do you want to go back to public school?"

"No."

"It's not for him to say, not at this particular moment, but he thinks you need to make something in school besides paragraphs."

"Like what? Bookshelves?"

"No. Not like that. Yourself."

"Somebody not like me, right?" Corey asked, and when his mother didn't answer, he was sure she'd received bad news at the clinic.

She beckoned him closer, and he bent down when she tilted her face up at him. "You should know," she whispered, "that your father was taking more than he put in near the end. It's the reason he got caught." When she gripped his shoulders and began to sob, Corey imagined she was evaluating his muscles while she cried.

* * *

Corey went to church by himself. One he could walk to. There were fewer pews, but all of the windows along each side were stained glass. And there were statues of Jesus and Mary, more than one of each, so it looked like a museum. Like they were valuable and one of a kind made so long ago nobody remembered where they'd been created.

He remembered his mother telling him the Catholics had been around a lot longer than the Lutherans. He sat in the back by himself, and after the sermon began, he started to look for people who looked different from those who went to the Lutheran church. Boys his age. Somebody missing a body part. Even the commonplace of enormously fat or scarily skinny.

Everybody looked normal. Nobody looked like a thief.

* * *

The next week his mother drove him toward Philadelphia again, this time to a place called Longwood Gardens. "Isn't this nice," she said. "And so close to us all these years without us going."

"Yeah," Corey said, but he didn't see how he was learning anything here where bushes were trimmed to look like animals.

"It's called topiary," she said. "There's a new word for you. " She stood in front of an enormous bush trimmed into the shape of a tyrannosaurus rex. "I know there's a lot going on in that brain of yours, but things will settle down soon. It's a wonder there's room for everything you're thinking, but I want you to write about this. Show me something beautiful with words."

"OK," he said, but it felt as if his head had begun to swell.

"I can't always find new places to see," she said. "You know that, don't you?"

"Yes." Corey thought she was going to tell him now—that her cancer had spread into places that were near the bottom of that list, how by next year he'd be in a public school and she'd be in a hospital or worse, but all she did was sit on a bench near a row of bushes shaped like the heads of children.

"Doesn't this beat all?" she said.

"Yes." Corey was ready to agree with anything she said because he wanted her to be happy. "Your father still has his job," she said, and then she went quiet, looking above those children's heads as if she expected to see the green bodies of adults.

"Your father thinks prayer works," she finally said. "He says the same words every night the way people say hello and goodbye and think they've gotten to know somebody."

Corey had wanted to pray for his father, but he couldn't think of any words but the ones from church, somebody else's. A prayer can't work, he thought, unless you make up the words yourself.

"You always think people can change," she said. "Even when they don't, you keep thinking it or else you end up in the dark."

Corey nodded. It was the same reason she was teaching him herself, so he wouldn't end up in the dark. It was why she didn't go to church. But all Corey could think of was how things must have looked when the whole world was in the dark before God said, "Let there be light." It was what everybody was afraid of, going back to where they'd come from.

THE PROPER WORDS FOR SIN

My son loves to watch me spray the DDT. "Good," he says, as I walk backwards, the cloud of mist following me around the house.

He hates bugs. All of them, even ladybugs and fireflies, the ones other children collect and carry in jars until those creatures die. It's gotten to keeping him inside more than a boy of near twelve ought to be, one about to finish sixth grade with a sister going on fourteen who brings home all the problems that come with that.

"If we lived in the South," I remind him when he wears me out with his squeamishness, "you'd find out what insects can become without weather to discourage them."

He shudders at that. For real. Like Alfalfa or one of those characters hamming it up in the *Little Rascals* reruns he watches, everything exaggerated so a dog would get what they were up to if it took a mind to watch television.

What's made it worse is this spring our new neighbors, the ones who arrived in March the day Kruschev's picture was on the front page because now he was in charge of the Soviets, are bookish. Forward about it, especially the father, who is all the time making a reference to something he's read, even if it's something we all know about from doing, and telling me, a milkman, about the danger in what every family ought to have on its dinner table. "Cream," he says, making the word sound like *cancer*. "You know, don't you, what that can do to you?"

While I'm spraying, he comes across the street without an invitation, like we've been friends for years. "This isn't good for anything," he says to me. "It's as bad as fallout."

"It's a miracle, is what it is," I say.

"A miracle will be if we're all still here in ten years. People forget the simplest things right in front of their faces. The food chain. Remember?"

I nod because I know I have to unless I want to look the idiot, but a little more comfort and a bit less nuisance seem a small thing to ask from this life, and there are scientists who know more than Kevin Naugle, who use the word *miracle* when they speak of DDT.

"Your boy will be accelerated, I hear," he says now, being what Naugle calls affable, and I nod at that. "And your daughter," I say, thinking that's what Naugle wants to hear.

"They're Sputnik children," he says. "The Soviets have shaken us awake."

We have something to agree on. Accelerated means pushed hard in science and math, ten percent of next year's seventh graders taking algebra and physical science, launching them toward college-level courses by their junior year. "If it helps the country, I'm all for it," I say, though I worry for my boy among the brainy.

"Your boy won't be a milkman," Naugle says. "Those days are about gone." I don't know exactly what Kevin Naugle does in his shirt and tie all day, but my wife, Mildred, has given him the advantage by telling him how I earn our bread and butter. I want to say a man in a tie standing outside at eight o'clock on a beautiful late May evening is a sorry thing, but I keep that to myself. My boy and his daughter have hit it off, a good thing, maybe, though I have my qualms.

Naugle's daughter looks to be a handful. Dressing in what looks like two sizes too small, her hair combed over one eye like she wants you to think she's mysterious. "She just wants to look like a movie star," my wife says, making excuses as soon as she hears me say she looks like she's hiding.

"Is that in style?" I ask, and when she says, "No," I say, "OK then."

Even my daughter, Elise, jokes that her brother's little friend needs to act her age. "She's twelve going on sixteen," she's said more than once, though I'm here to say that girl, Carol is her name, has a voice on the phone that makes me wish I were twelve. It's musical, which sounds silly to put into words, but there's nothing else for describing it. "Is Billy there?" she says, sounding like she's starting up the do-re-mis, and I call him, finding myself using my after-church voice just so she knows how civil we are here.

When Billy takes the phone, he waits for me to leave the kitchen before he starts to talk. I hear her laugh, and I imagine that girl talking about rock and roll singers and such, turning Billy's head away from the things boys ought to be doing.

"You should have boys as friends," I've said. "You should be practicing baseball in between your league games."

He plays shortstop most games, where one of the best players always plays, but he never practices, swinging a bat only just before and during games. It's been a year since he caught balls with me in the yard. It's his final summer before Pony League, when pitchers throw curve balls, when batting practice is a must. Already, he acts as if this will be the last year he plays a game that he's always been good at.

Tonight, Billy writes on the pad by the phone while he talks, taking notes as if he were in school. After he hangs up, I notice him lift the dictionary off the shelf in the den and start up the stairs. I ask him right out what he wants with it now that school is down to its last week. "Looking up things," he says. "Carol's so smart. She knows all these words."

"Like what?"

"Words I never heard of."

I wait, but he doesn't go on. After he closes his door, I try to make out the words by what's come through on the next page of the note-pad, but aside from seeing the words are uniformly long, I can't make them out. I think of that girl, her brains and the way she shows herself, and I think: fornication, cunnilingus, and fellatio.

I've seen that girl in her room. She leaves her drapes open. I've seen her unbutton her blouse and flash her new white bra, and when she lifts it off her chest, her small breasts are so firm-looking there's no question she doesn't need the bra for anything but keeping her nipples from showing through the tight sweaters and blouses she wears. I think of my son down the hall, how he might be watching, how she might be doing this for him, that she's been giving him the proper words for sin so he knows what he has to pick from, starting with voyeur, while this girl undoes her clothes like somebody who enjoys it.

While I watch, I think that maybe my son is right this second un-dressing for her, though I've never seen her glance this way. Could someone be so convincingly naïve? She's hidden below the waist, but he'd be visible, and so would I, if I turned on the light and let her see it was a man watching her and what she could expect to see in return if she kept at her behavior.

* * *

My wife is home all day, but she doesn't spend time with the neigh-bor women. Mildred has the television to keep her company, and I'm home by three, what with the milk going out early like it needs to. So she turns it off at 3:30, as soon as some woman gets into difficulty on *The Secret Storm*. I usually watch a few minutes near the end, wondering how so much misfortune can settle on one person, but when school ends, there's Billy sitting beside her like somebody's wife. I frown at Mildred, but I wait until the beautiful woman who might have multiple sclerosis waits for the doctor's report.

"He's not sitting here all day," Mildred says at once, so she knows what I'm thinking. "It's half an hour. It's good for the boy to see he's well off compared to some." I give her a look that reminds her it's summer and the middle of the afternoon, a time when only housewives or old women are watching, when a boy should be judging the flight of a baseball off a bat.

*   *   *

"So many things can go wrong," he says at dinner after two weeks of watching, making him sound as if he's been watching *The Secret Storm* for years instead of taking in only ten afternoons of claptrap.

"Trouble is like insects," I tell him. "It's everywhere. That's why we have the DDT. You'll see. In a few years you'll hardly see a bug. They're licked. They just don't know it yet."

"No, they're not. They can adapt faster than we can kill them."

"Who are you talking to? You're not getting this in school, that's for sure."

Elise smiles as if she has a secret. "What has you in stitches?" I say.

"Before he got so smart, Billy was getting himself in a sweat about bugs getting born straight out of dog dirt. You know old man Miller next door has those two retrievers, and their yard is full of it."

I look at Billy, who's glaring at his sister as if he wants to dump the bowl of green beans over her head. "Spontaneous generation," he says. "Smart people believed in it once."

"Where'd you hear that?" I ask.

"Mr. Naugle. He says Aristotle thought he proved it. He had good reasons to not get it right. He didn't have microscopes. He watched mud and feces with just his bare eyes."

"He watched feces, did he? There's a job for a man in a shirt and tie."

"Can you imagine anybody believing that for even one second?" Elise says. "You'd have to be a total moron."

"Shush now," Mildred says, but she gives Billy a puzzled look. "I thought Kevin Naugle was a man of science. He sounds more like a fundamentalist."

Billy shrugs. "It was Mr. Naugle's idea of a joke, Mom. He had me going for a while. He was scaring me. He knows I hate bugs, and he had me starting to think they could come from anywhere that was warm and damp and dirty."

"Never mind him," Mildred says, but Billy acts as if she hasn't said a word, so I know he's past the embarrassing part of the story.

"You know what's scary for real?" he says. "It doesn't matter that bugs don't come from mud. All the DDT in the world can't kill them because there will always be some that can live with the poison, and then their children will be even harder to kill."

I take a bite of meat loaf. I don't have to argue. I'm not the one who's afraid of insects. Mildred isn't eating. Her expression hasn't changed. "I still don't understand why anybody would tell a story like that as a joke," she says. "It's like saying Zeus is watching us and has decided to change us into spiders or trees."

"Who's Zeus?" Elise says, and Billy looks at her triumphantly.

"You're the moron," Billy says, though when she hisses, in return, "Science boy," not raising her voice, it sounds like the worst sort of dismissal.

* * *

Most mornings, once I'm in the truck and on my route, work calms me. I love the first hour of driving when it's still half-dark, even in summer, and there's hardly even a car to pass. There's so much promise in that emptiness and light, as if life has shifted for the better, and I think that maybe some morning the first person I see will look changed, and I'll know from now on things will be different.

And there is a pleasure in retrieving empties and replacing them in the milk box slots with glass bottles full to the brim. There are still people on the route who prefer glass, and I imagine them to be people I want to know. Milk's better in glass. It's not a thing improved by convenience. I've been drinking milk from bottles so long I wouldn't want it to come another way. And all that wax on the paper cartons—it gets onto things. And a man like Kevin Naugle would remind you it makes more trash, though you don't need science to see it's a waste. I tell myself to mention it the next time I see him, create a little bit of friendly agreement, but then I think of him predicting the end of milkmen, and I know I won't say a word.

Just one customer cancels during July. A man like Naugle would take that the wrong way, ask me when was the last time someone was added to my route, but I don't see much of my neighbor, and then some good things happen to the country near the end of July, not the least of which, NASA gets started so the U.S. can get serious about beating the Soviets. "About time," I tell Billy while I drive him to his last Little League game. "Now we're cooking with gas."

"It's not a race, Dad," he says, looking out the side window as if he's never seen the road we live on before.

"The hell it's not," I say, but he doesn't answer.

By ten days later, when Eisenhower announces that the Nautilus has gone under the North Pole, meaning the Russians know we can send a submarine anywhere at any time, Billy has a habit of going over to the Naugles' every day to listen to records with the little firecracker. I can hear those songs coming across the street from their screened-in front porch. I can see the both of them moving around, but I can't hear their voices, even between the Everly Brothers and Elvis and Buddy Holly.

They keep their voices low or maybe they don't talk, but part of the problem with my paying attention is that Elise and her friends stand in the yard every afternoon swinging their hips to keep hula hoops twirling. "That's something they're too old to be doing," I say to Mildred when *The Secret Storm* is over and Billy is across the street.

"They're just being girls," she says. "They're only fourteen."

"It's not their age I'm talking about," I say, and she brushes past me.

"You keep your eyes in your head, then," she nearly spits.

And then, for three straight days, Billy stays in the house after *The Secret Storm*. "Your friend go to summer camp?" I ask him.

"No," he says.

"What then?"

"She wants to be by herself."

I give him a nod of acknowledgement. "You'll be seeing a lot of girls in a few weeks."

"We're not boyfriend/girlfriend, Dad," he says. "You think you know something, but you don't."

* * *

After another month of him holed up in his room or across the street, I'm happy when school starts again, but on the second day of junior high, Billy comes home from school with a story about being humiliated on the bus. A senior, he says, took his gym bag and opened it, pulling out his brand new gym suit, the one with a dog's head on the t-shirt and a matching one on the shorts. He tossed it on the floor and held up the once-used jock strap. "Medium," the boy read from the label inside the waistband, and then he said, "Your little prick and peanuts couldn't fill this."

My son quotes the boy like I'm a policeman. I'm surprised Billy humiliates himself a second time and wish he would summarize, or better, keep the whole thing to himself. "Sit in the front of the bus," I say. "You can't fight boys five years older than you are."

"I don't want to fight him, Dad," he says. "I want to kill him."

"I understand," I say, but my son's tone is so even he sounds like somebody who wishes I kept guns around the house.

"You don't," he says. "What if Elise had her bra tossed around the bus? What would you tell her to do?"

Cover yourself, I think, but I shake my head slowly and say, "It won't happen again. You'll see. Boys like that won't even notice you if you keep to yourself."

"32B—that's what that guy would yell out about Elise. He'd tell everybody how big her breasts were."

My son starts to cry. Twelve years old now and he sobs in a way that makes me want to say, "Grow up," as if I am somebody who doesn't give a damn whether his son will hate him after he hears those words.

I don't know my wife's bra size, let alone my daughter's. Small, medium, large—the sizes for men and boys are easy, but to have your body measured so explicitly is an awkward thing to get around.

"That's not going to happen to Elise," I say. "Don't you worry about that."

* * *

The next afternoon he doesn't come home after school. "He's watching *American Bandstand* with Carol Naugle," Mildred says.

"Is it a special?" I ask.

"It's on every day, George. He's been going over there for quite a while, if you haven't noticed, and now that school started, he asked me for permission. Here, see for yourself."

She turns the television back on, and I watch two lines of boys and girls clapping their hands while couples shuffle between them. "He wants to watch kids dance?" I say.

"I'm happy he's taken to this. Maybe he'll learn to dance," she says. "This one's called 'The Stroll.' I think all you have to do is look cool walking when it's your turn."

When the record ends, a slow song begins, and the teenagers pair up to embrace. "I like this one," I say. "I've heard this somewhere."

"It's Tommy Edwards," she says. "It's really popular." I watch the couples as the song plays until Mildred gets up from the chair and turns it off.

"That's enough for one day," she says. "It's for kids, not for us."

"I know where I've heard it," I say. "Elise plays that song. She sits in her room and sings along the way she does to Pat Boone and Johnny Mathis and all the rest."

Mildred frowns. "I thought you meant that you'd heard it some-place else."

* * *

In the middle of September, Naugle's daughter misses school for a week, something neither of my children have ever done. "That's twice in one month," I say.

"She's sick," Mildred says on the fifth day. "Maybe she has horrible cramps. You know what happens to girls at her age."

I can hear *American Bandstand* playing in the basement. I listen for a moment, trying to hear if Billy is shuffling his feet to the music. "Maybe she doesn't have the get up and go to look the world in the eye."

"What's that supposed to mean?"

I twist a finger near my right temple and grimace, and my wife says, "She's just growing up. If you paid attention to your daughter, you'd know."

"I don't see Elise staying in bed all day."

"That's foolishness talking, Jack. If ever I heard it." She looks toward the basement as if she expects Billy to be eavesdropping. "You should hope your children don't pay their father any mind when it comes to knowing what's in the heart," she says, and I spin and leave the room before I find myself telling her if she opened her eyes she'd see the world didn't look anything like what she pretended, and to say otherwise made you a moron.

That night Billy calls me downstairs where he's been hiding himself every night now that there's no phone calls. "Dad!" he shouts. "Dad!" As if a fire has started, I think, hurrying down the steps to where he's standing beside his chair, turned away from where the television shows photographs of the evening sky. I follow his eyes to a millipede halfway up the wall. "Spray it," he says, but I know better than to fill the room with a cloud in order to kill just one crawling thing. I take a Kleenex from the box Mildred keeps on an end table and pinch the millipede into a small blot surrounded by tiny legs.

Billy turns slowly, examining the walls. "There's more, right?" he says.

"You can count on it."

"I can't watch TV down here then."

"Just when it's dark. They don't come out in daylight. They know what's good for them. What with the lights on, I don't know what got into this one."

On the screen a man in a dark suit is pointing at a model of the solar system. "It was huge," Billy says.

"For a millipede," I say. "He probably thought he was a tough guy when he was behind the wall."

"He should have stopped there then. Being big gets you into trouble." When Billy goes on, explaining that he wishes he wasn't so tall, I tell him he's lucky, that he'll fill out and be strong and glad for it.

"No," he says. "That's the problem. If you're big, you're always expected to be tough. If you're small, you have a choice."

"Tough comes with being big," I say, but looking at him, I don't believe it at all, and my son shakes his head at once.

So he turns off the television just as the man in the suit holds up the model as if it is a brand new baby, and God's truth, I'm happy, for once, with his squeamishness because he's watching WQED, the education channel in our city. I remember watching one of their shows for a few minutes once and wondering who would sit down with something that was so much like school. Somebody like Kevin Naugle, I think now. Somebody who was still dressed for work even though it was dark outside.

* * *

On Monday, Billy goes directly to the Naugles' house after school, and that night, when I answer the phone, I hear "Mr. Enright. Hi, there," that girl's voice as musical as ever, nothing like somebody should sound after she's been sick so long.

I've never heard that girl's voice clear enough for words except on the phone. When I see her outside she always waves, a small, fingertip-flutter like she's saying hello as she stands over a crib. I think about that music, whether she will always sound like that. Maybe a girl's voice changes like a boy's sometimes, though my own daughter sounds no different, beginning high school, than she did in sixth grade.

They talk for half an hour, as long as one of those science shows on television, and an hour later, when I go into the bedroom, there she is big as life undressing like she hasn't been out of sight for a week.

Carol Naugle is a 32A—the number comes to me as if it's been shouted down the aisle by a school bully. The girl is as thin as my daughter, but her breasts are smaller, and unless there is a size smaller than A, I know what is printed on the bra she slips off.

All boys must watch like this, I think. They look in windows for a glimpse of the world to come. They hope for their sister's door to be ajar, for the perfect timing that places them outside that door at the moment when a blouse slides off shoulders, when a skirt drops to the floor. I saw my sister just once like that and never said a word to anyone, but I listened to all of the stories told by classmates in junior high school, especially the week-by-week story one boy told throughout eighth grade about watching his neighbor, of sitting in the dark and waiting because that girl, thirteen, undressed at 10:30 every night.

While that girl reaches for her pajamas, I slip down the hall and go to my son's room, but Billy is in bed with his eyes closed.

I wonder how fast he can get into bed if he hears me coming, but when I walk closer, I think he's really asleep, that Naugle's daughter is putting on a show, and he's not watching. I remember Elise saying "science boy," the phrase sounding terrible. When I look across the street, I notice, for the first time, that she has a television in her bedroom.

* * *

As if he's caught something from that girl, a week later my son stays home from school for three straight days. When I come home the third day, he's watching *The Secret Storm* with Mildred as if it's summer. The women on this episode seem to be an especially sad lot. One is pregnant. One has cancer. And one has a husband who's set fire to her house. When the show ends, that woman is screaming for the firemen to search inside the burning house for her husband, who she thinks is asleep, but we know he's out drinking in a bar to set up an alibi. "Isn't that something?" Mildred says, standing and going upstairs before I can tell her that the husband will be caught for sure, that no sin is left unpunished in these shows.

Billy smiles when the show ends, and I think for a moment he's been fooled into thinking the husband is trapped inside the burning house, getting what he deserves, but he tells me the boy who opened his gym bag the first week of school was in a fight on the bus while Carol Naugle was absent and was beaten up by a boy who sits in the last seat, alone, every day. "Cy Griffin," Billy says. "He never talks to anybody. He never has a book in his hand. All of a sudden he has Bill Markle over a seat and is punching his face. He broke his nose, Dad. He must have. It was all bloody. The driver stopped the bus and told them both to get off, and everybody could see Cy punching him some more by the side of the road."

Some goodness comes to the world, I think, but my son is flushed with telling me. "It was like he was killing him, Dad. It was great. I was hoping he'd throw him under the back wheels."

I say, "Slow down, there. He got his beating. That's enough."

My son makes boxing motions with his arms, uppercuts and hooks. "You know what Cy Griffin is?" he says. "He's like a genius or something. When he reads a book, he remembers every word."

"Photographic memory?"

"Yeah. There's a better word for it. I thought he maybe couldn't even read because he never had a book, but it's just the opposite. A genius and a fighter."

"Why didn't you tell me this when it happened?"

"It's only been a week, Dad. I told Carol. It cheered her up to hear about somebody getting what they deserved. She went back to school the next day. You saw."

He tells me he's going across the street. "Three days off," I say. "I thought you were really sick."

"I was. But I'm better now."

"Who's on *American Bandstand* today? Elvis? Buddy Holly?"

"We stopped watching last week," Billy says. "Carol says it's stupid to watch people pretend to be singing." Before I can ask what they do instead, he's gone.

* * *

"Here's a story for you," Naugle says, coming across the street when he sees me doing my last spray before the weather turns cold. "A long time ago, where they grew mandarin oranges in southern China, the farmers had problems with insects. Nobody had ever heard of DDT, but they paid attention, and after a while, they decided to hang bags of yellow ants in the trees. They laid bamboo bridges from tree to tree to let them spread, and those ants ate the insects that ate the oranges."

"If it was that easy, there'd be something eating mosquitoes."

Naugle doesn't change his expression. "The Chinese protected frogs; they revered the praying mantis. You can figure out why."

"I get it."

"They had a certain kind of leaf they put into books that kept bookworms from destroying them. They got things done without poison."

"For all that, the Chinese don't seem to be doing very well," I say. "They're miserable and Communist at the same time. And the ones who live in the South, they have malaria to deal with. DDT will save their lives."

"You know what will come of that?" Naugle says. "More people than the world can stand. Malaria has always been like birth control in those places."

* * *

"What are you doing in here?" my wife says, startling me. I never thought she could approach the bedroom without me hearing her. She switches on the overhead light, and I squint like a man who's been in the dark for longer than a few seconds. "I was thinking," I say. "The dark helps me to concentrate."

Her eyes go to the window she's looked out a thousand times, the view so familiar I trust she won't recognize which part of it I was watching unless the girl has entered her room in the past ten seconds and begun to undress.

"You should go for a walk then. The darkness along with moving your body is better. Standing here is like watching a turned off television. You've seen this so many times it might as well be blank."

"I guess. But every once in a while I like to look outside at night."

She doesn't smile. Her lips are set tightly straight across her face—like the lips of a stick figure, I think, like one drawn with just one line from side to side.

She moves past me and pulls the drapes shut, adjusting the ends so they meet exactly. "As soon as the lights are on, these go shut," she says. "Otherwise I feel naked."

"How do you feel when you go outside and there aren't any drapes?"

"You know what I mean."

* * *

"There was a show on television today about DDT," Billy says. "You know what the letters stand for?"

"No idea."

"Isn't it a brand name?" Mildred says.

"DichloroDiphenylTrichloroethane," Billy says, sounding like he's giving an answer on *The $64,000 Question.*

"No wonder they changed the name then," Mildred says.

"It's white crystal, Dad. It doesn't have any odor or taste. It doesn't dissolve very fast but at least it breaks down quickly in the sun."

"At least?"

"So the poison goes away faster."

"I'll spray on a cloudy day next time."

"We should know what everything is made of, Dad. It's important."

"Like soap?" I say. "It works. We're clean. That's enough to know."

"For everything. You don't know whether or not some soap isn't as good for you as another."

"We know milk is good for us," I say. "So we drink it."

My son shakes his head, and I feel the fear that precedes rage, like when I'd lost my job with the highway department because a county commissioner had been voted out of office. "Mr. Naugle says we shouldn't be so sure about milk. He says it's only a matter of time before the world wises up."

"Good luck to your Mr. Naugle when his bones start to break."

"Carol doesn't drink milk."

"She'll regret it," Elise suddenly says. "She'll get a hump like old Mrs. Shelby down the street."

"She doesn't eat meat either."

Elise taps her slice of roast beef with her fork. "What does she do, graze?"

I smile at her. "You like that song 'It's All in the Game'?" I ask.

She makes a face. "That's so old now. I wish the radio would quit playing it."

"How about you?" I say to Billy.

"I've never heard it, Dad."

Elise makes another face. "It's been number one for a month. You're as weird as your little friend."

That night, when Naugle's daughter calls, Billy hangs up in a minute. "What's wrong?" I say, as he heads for the door.

"She wants me to come over, Dad."

"That's new."

"The telephone isn't good for some things."

As soon as he leaves, I go upstairs, but neither of them enter the girl's bedroom. I listen for Mildred for a moment, and then I walk to Billy's room and open my son's drawers, looking under his sweaters and t-shirts and underwear, hoping to find a lingerie catalogue slipped upstairs or maybe a *Playboy* borrowed from a friend whose father subscribes. His shirts look large enough for me to wear, and yet I outweigh my son by fifty pounds, maybe more. They make him look even skinnier, like a bag of bones, the phrase coming back to me from my own days in seventh grade.

I don't find anything. Not in his drawers or under his mattress or deep in his closet. It's the room of a nine-year-old. The dictionary by the bed is the only odd thing in the room, and I carry it into the hall where there's light, open it, and leaf through until I reach Pederasty: *Sodomy between males, especially as practiced by a man with a boy.* I turn to Sodomy: *Any sexual intercourse held to be abnormal, specifically anal intercourse between two male persons.* I imagine my son sitting in bed to read this, and then I try to imagine a twelve-year-old boy looking up Naugle's science words, even if they were delivered by the sweetest telephone voice in the United States. Sodium fluoroacetate is at the top of sodomy's column: *A powder used as a rodent poison,* the dictionary says. And then comes sodium hydroxide, hypochlorite, and hyposulfite, and I think of Cy Griffin memorizing definitions like this, put the dictionary back, walk outside, and cut through the backyard into the housing plan where Billy has told me Griffin and the boy he'd thrashed both live.

I pass eight houses before I see anyone outside, and then, just as I hear music, I see two boys and a girl who look like they might be seniors in high school. My son has said the tough boy has a DA, and both of these boys do. Cy Griffin, he's told me, has a Marine cut. Both boys are tall and thick, football player types who'd rather spend their time working on cars and drinking beer and chasing girls like the one sitting on the steps beside six empty bottles. The steps run up to a small porch like the one attached to every house on this street, all of them built within a few years of each other less than ten years ago.

I think of one of these boys being pounded and give credit to Cy Griffin for being truly frightening. And I can't imagine my son, in five years, resembling either of these boys, let alone Cy Griffin.

I pass thirty-three more houses, but no one else is visible, and when I step out onto the street and turn left toward our street, I exhale like I've just managed a gauntlet of muggers.

*　*　*

Soon Naugle's daughter misses another two days of school. "Check the calendar," I say to Mildred. "It's not what you say it is." She puts a finger to her lips, but Billy goes upstairs as if he doesn't hear me.

Before midnight, an ambulance pulls into Naugle's driveway. Mildred and I watch from the window. The lights are on in the daughter's room, but the drapes are closed. We follow the shadows of what must be the attendants, and then Mildred goes to Billy's room. When she doesn't come back in a minute, I know he's awake and watching.

"She swallowed Drano," Mildred says when I get home from my route the next day. Billy sits beside her on the couch; Elise is rocking in the chair Mildred bought for herself when she found out she was pregnant for the first time.

So I was right, I keep myself from saying. That girl is someone who gets sick just from waking up in the morning. I look at Mildred to gauge whether or not the girl is alive, but Billy volunteers, "She won't be able to eat like a normal person, not for a long time or maybe ever."

Mildred sighs in a way I think the women who watch afternoon television would appreciate. "There's no fixing the damage something like that does," she says. When no one else speaks, she adds, "She'll need watching."

"It's so creepy to think about," Elise says. "She'll always be weird now."

I go outside to walk in the yard, and I'm surprised Billy follows me. We end up at the edge of the backyard where we can look past the junipers toward the housing plan where Cy Griffin and the gym-bag boy are just home from school like my children. Billy stares between his shoes for a minute, while I wait. "There's no bugs," he finally says.

"It's the DDT," I say, but my son shakes his head.

"It's just getting cold," he says. "That's all it is. They'll all be back—like baseball."

"Maybe she'll heal," I say. "There's probably not much experience with this sort of thing to predict from." When he doesn't answer, I ask, "Can she talk?"

"Talk? She can't even eat now."

"There's two pipes going down, aren't there?"

"She was going to have to move again," my son says.

"They've only been here six months."

"That's just it. She wanted to stay here."

"A child doesn't get much say in something like that."

"She's not a baby, Dad." My son stares away from me. I see his hands are both clenched, and think, for a moment, he is fighting the impulse to attack me.

* * *

When the girl comes home a few weeks later, Mildred walks over with a casserole, but Billy goes downstairs to the television, leaving the lights off as if he wants the millipedes to attack. I watch the girl's room, and there is a light on, but the drapes are drawn, and that light is so dim I know it is leaking in from the hallway, that the girl is lying in the dark with the door open so her parents can look in on her every time they pass by. There isn't going to be any privacy in that house for a long time, that's for sure. No doors being closed by children.

I think of Kevin Naugle preaching about poisons yet keeping Drano in the house, pouring it down his sink like he's forgotten where the water goes. You can unscrew an elbow pipe in a few seconds. You can get yourself down under the sink and work at it. That's where you'll find the clog. Every time. And then you pull the gunk out of there and reconnect the pipe and everything's good as new.

Drano is for the lazy. A pipe's one thing, not a million, like bugs. You can't squash one of them and walk away smiling. Kevin Naugle has no sense about anything. You have to pick your fights and take the best tack. It's how we get along in the world. It's how we make do.

We get what we deserve, I think, imagining Kevin Naugle discovering the evil in his science, his sins of pride being punished through his daughter. And I'll admit it's an evil thought in its own self, but then there comes riding up the knowing that I have troubles in my own house and all of them well deserved. So there is no gloating about any of what is in my head and won't shake loose. I remember that girl's musical voice, and that is something, and I can believe, at least for a while longer, that some sort of better luck might befall us, because otherwise we'll have to childproof our house like we're parents to sons and daughters who cannot help themselves.

YOU CAN LOOK THIS UP

"THIS IS YOUR UNCLE JACK," the voice on the phone said, and Len Phelps hesitated long enough to hear, "Your father's brother," before he managed to answer, "OK."

Uncle Jack kept his own silence then. Paused like a schoolboy getting up the courage to ask for a date. "Your Aunt Harriet said I should call."

Phelps was trying to remember when he'd last spoken to Uncle Jack. His father's funeral, probably, a thank you for his condolences in a crowded room. Surely not more than two sentences and twenty-eight years ago for that.

Before then? Not since high school, forty years now. He'd be hard pressed to pick Uncle Jack out of a lineup.

He talked to Aunt Harriet once a year. She'd told him about Uncle Jack fainting, how his symptoms seemed identical to Phelps's father's two weeks before he died. She'd put the fear in Uncle Jack with that allusion, Phelps thought, but why on earth she'd sent Uncle Jack to him instead of a doctor was a puzzle Uncle Jack needed to solve for him. Uncle Jack had plenty of money. He had a condo on Hilton Head. He belonged to a country club.

"I've had these fainting spells," Uncle Jack finally said. "Two times, just like Ed did back then before he passed."

"He needed bypass surgery."

"What do you think I should do?"

"See your doctor." So it was that easy. A sentence of common sense.

Uncle Jack went quiet again, and Phelps, when he took the receiver from his ear, heard a roar from his downstairs television, a bad sign, since the Pirates were playing in Cincinnati. "I'm worried," Uncle Jack finally said. "I don't know what to do."

"That's what the doctor's for."

"You think it might be serious? I'm seventy-six years old. Ed was what, sixty-two, sixty-three?"

"Fifty-nine." Phelps could hear a commercial begin. A pitching change, he thought. A disaster early in the game.

"I feel just fine except for those blackouts."

"Good. Maybe it's something else."

"That's what I was thinking. You never can tell."

"Exactly." Phelps waited, but Uncle Jack didn't speak. Phelps counted to twenty before he said, "OK, then," and hung up.

* * *

It had been so long since his father had died that Phelps had had time to develop heart problems of his own. Uncle Jack could count himself lucky living to seventy-six with nothing but health, until he tumbled to the ground on the fourteenth tee at his country club. Phelps was fifty-seven and thinking every flight of stairs was a bullet.

Two years ago he'd had a heart attack in one of his classes at the community college. Business Writing. They were learning the intricacies of the job application letter. They'd finished with the colon after the greeting, how this showed formality and respect and a sense of what the world expected from you if you wanted to work with your brain instead of your hands.

Just as he started in on the crucial first paragraph, how it introduced the employer to the applicant's qualifications and interest, Phelps had felt tightness in his chest and his voice had squeaked shut. There was no surprise when pain ran down his arm. "Oh Christ," he thought, "not here in front of the computer geeks," just before he was lost in the inability to do anything but sit and go helpless.

He'd done better than his friend George Aikey, who'd had an aneurysm burst in class on the first day of the semester, a room full of strangers hovering over his dead body five minutes after he'd taken roll. A mild attack, Phelps's doctor had said. A warning. A wake up call.

The doctor talked like that, in threes. "How are you? How you doing? Feeling OK?" Phelps wanted to answer, "Enough of that. Stop it. Shut up." Instead, he kept that triple play to himself like everything else, including his conviction that a mild attack was like a civil defense alarm minutes before the first nuclear missile arced over the horizon.

Phelps had a son of his own who needed to listen up about his future. Thirty-three years old—it wouldn't be long before Drew remembered every chicken wing and cheeseburger as he climbed a flight of stairs. Like his grandfather, Drew believed not smoking and avoiding custard pie was the cornerstone of a healthy lifestyle while he grew heavy on pizza and cheese steaks and nightly movie rentals.

His son worked night shift at the Hampton Inn. "It's good for me," Drew had explained once, describing how he read most of the time after midnight and had access to the hotel's fitness room. For the past two years he'd been building himself up with the free weights. "I go in at 4 a.m. when nobody ever comes in or goes out. I watch the news while I lift. It comes around twice every half hour. Sometimes it seems to be identical, but if you pay attention, there are small things that change."

* * *

An hour after Uncle Jack called, the Pirates down by seven runs in the sixth inning, Phelps left early for the restaurant where he was meeting Drew for dinner. He sat at the bar with a beer that came in a glass that reminded him of a bowling pin. The bartender claimed it held twenty-three ounces of beer, but the shape discouraged verification. By the time Drew entered, Phelps was working on an ordinary sixteen-ounce mug he carried to where his son was confirming their reservation. "Hey," he said, "thought I'd order a beer while I was waiting."

"I'm starved," Drew said. After the waitress came to their table, after Phelps ordered another beer and a Santa Fe salad, Drew ordered three appetizers for dinner—a dozen clams, a cheese quesadilla, and eighteen wings. "Bring them one at a time," Drew said. When Phelps frowned, Drew added, "This way I don't get any of the stuff I never eat."

"Vegetables?"

"And salads. They always come with dinners."

"The all meat diet?"

"And bread. And there's tomatoes in the salsa."

"And dairy in cheese."

"See?"

To Phelps's dismay, Drew sipped his water through the straw the restaurant unaccountably provided. He drained his beer, imagining, with every gulp, how awful it would taste through a straw.

"Remember how you always used to say 'eat the meat' when we were stuffed?" Drew said, still holding the straw between two fingers. "We had to fish it out of the sandwich and finish it. You never said eat the bun or eat the French fries, but we had to finish the burger like it was a cookie."

"I got that from my father."

"There you go."

At last, Drew let go of the straw, growing up before Phelps's eyes. "You're thirty-three now. You have another ten years, maybe, before this catches up with you."

"So I better enjoy it now."

"That's the spirit."

"Yes it is." The waitress placed the wings, eighteen of them shiny with grease and sauce, in front of Drew. Phelps ordered another beer.

"Your Uncle Jack called today. Right out of nowhere. He thinks he's dying."

"He's the rich uncle, right?"

"He lives like it, at least."

Drew dipped a wing into the tub of blue cheese dressing on his plate and held it up like a commercial for cholesterol. "I don't think I ever told you about this guy last week who came into the fitness room a few minutes after I started. He wasn't dressed for the gym. He said he wanted to watch television. Said he didn't want to wake up his wife. He asked if he could change the channel. He had a bag of cookies with him—you know, Oreos. I knew the movie; I knew it was about over when I finished my workout, so I just got on the stationary bike and pedaled at low resistance and let the movie end before I closed up. I should do some aerobics maybe. It was only the second time I was ever on that bike. The guy threw the bag away as he left. He didn't even take a drink of water from the cooler."

"How many cookies are in a bag like that?"

"Forty-six."

"You know something like that?"

"I ate half a bag once. I remember it was twenty-three. I made my-self stop, but I counted the ones in the other side to see the damage."

Phelps's salad arrived with Drew's quesadilla, and he nudged his half-empty beer into the center of the table. "And he's the only person who's ever been in there with you?"

"So far. I've only worked there six months. Which reminds me—you want to come cheer for me when I'm in a doughnut eating contest at the county fair?"

Phelps watched Drew guide the melted cheese that oozed from the side of the quesadilla into his mouth. "You mean like all you can eat?"

"In eight minutes."

Maybe it wasn't so bad, Phelps thought. Eight minutes. How much damage could you do to yourself in eight minutes? "I've been watching eating contests," his son said, "getting a handle on technique."

"Where do you watch?"

"On television. They have these things on all the time."

"At least you won't choke to death," Phelps said, "but the last thing you need is eight minutes of doughnuts."

Drew sipped his water for so long that Phelps wanted to reach across the table and yank the straw out of his mouth. And then, his face still tilted toward the glass, Drew said, "Didn't you eat goldfish once?"

"Minnows. I was drunk and nineteen. They didn't have any cholesterol."

"Like father, like son," Drew said, putting his lips to the straw again, and Phelps expected him to blow bubbles, begin to babble *cooties* and *boogers* and *zizzits*, words never used after the age of ten. *It takes one to know one*, he thought. *Poop. Pee-pee.*

He remembered Drew, as a third grader, counting the empty cans of beer in the recycling bin by the refrigerator, and how, feeling guilty, he'd begun to put one out of every three cans directly into the garbage to lessen the total. Shortly after, his son had stopped announcing ten or eleven or twelve, and he'd understood that his son had seen the cans in the garbage and been driven to silence by his deception.

"You know what the record for doughnut eating is?" Drew said, finally sitting up to attack the rest of the quesadilla.

"Somebody keeps track?"

"There's an organization that sanctions these things. The International Federation of Competitive Eating."

Phelps calculated. "Thirty-two," he guessed. "That's four doughnuts per minute. Some fat ass could do that."

"Forty-nine," Drew said. "Glazed like the ones we're going to eat. They practically melt in your mouth." The clams, inexplicably, arrived last. Poking through a mound of lettuce for bits of chicken or cheese, Phelps fought the urge to order another beer. Drew, he noticed, was watching his fork. "How old do you have to be to just say the hell with it and go back to eating whatever you want?"

"I don't think it works like that. People don't think their lives are over and go on eating binges."

"They should. Let's say you're seventy-six like Uncle Jack. Why not eat wings and steaks and whatever you really like every night?"

His son, Phelps realized, was serious. "Because he wouldn't make it to seventy-seven."

"There's a year out there you're not going to reach."

"Anyway, food like that would make you sick when you're seventy-six. Guaranteed."

Drew held up a clam dripping with melted butter and looked at it thoughtfully. "So there," he said, as if some great truth had been revealed.

* * *

To learn what Drew was in for, Phelps watched the Coney Island Fourth of July hot dog eating contest on ESPN. The announcers acted as if this were a sport, something to train for, something soon to be added to the enormous list of sports at every high school. The winner, it turned out, wasn't any of the fat men who'd entered. A thin Japanese guy trounced everybody; the runner-up was a woman.

As soon as the show ended, Phelps logged on to look up the organization Drew had mentioned and, sure enough, there was a long list of records. A handful of names reappeared again and again. One woman owned records for asparagus, bratwurst, cheesecake, chicken nuggets, and chicken wings (167 in thirty-two minutes). He imagined gorging himself at that rate for even ten minutes, finishing off his heart for good in a brief ecstasy of grease and pepper.

His favorite was the category of "buffet food." Five and a half pounds of it stuffed down in twelve minutes. Phelps visualized a long table with bins of mashed potatoes and cloverleaf rolls and bread stuffing. Fried chicken. Roast beef. Ham. Phelps remembered stuffing himself as a teenager, his father bragging to his friends about how many trips he'd made to the buffet table at a restaurant called the Horn of Plenty.

There seemed to be heroism in overeating. His father, once, had said eating fettuccine alfredo was no different than riding a motorcycle. "What's the point of getting up in the morning if you worry so much?" he'd said. "You might as well wake up dead." Phelps had heard that expression a hundred times, but never outside of his family. It was like some characteristic passed down through generations, the shape of a nose, a talent for the sorts of puzzles that separated the quick-witted from the slow.

Wake up dead, he repeated to himself as Drew finished his clams. Phelps felt dizzy the way he did standing up quickly when he'd been drinking. He wanted the subject changed, but nothing came to him except the strange, distant voice of Uncle Jack.

* * *

Early the following morning, as Phelps was eating a bowl of cereal, Aunt Harriet called. "Did your Uncle Jack phone you?" she began and kept on as if he'd answered. "He told me he did, but I'm checking to be sure what with him telling me about his problems sounding just like Ray before he passed."

"Yes."

"And you knew right off who he was?"

"He said he was Uncle Jack."

"His voice, I mean. His manner. If it's family, it sticks to you like fly paper."

"I guess."

"You know who I am when I call, don't you? I don't need an introduction."

Aunt Harriet lived by herself in a trailer. Phelps had visited her once, and though she'd been an ordinary-sized woman and it had only been three years ago, he thought, listening to her voice, she'd grown fat. He imagined her struggling on the two makeshift wooden steps up to her trailer's door. There wasn't a railing. They'd been temporary but became permanent the way things did. "Did he go to the doctor?" Phelps said.

"That's what I'm calling about. Did it sound like he had his mind made up?"

"He was weighing things."

"That Jack," she said, "he's so skinny he can't believe his heart will stop, but you mark my words, he'll wake up dead some day just like your father."

"Maybe not."

"And you with your problems. You know the score."

"The doctor keeps my scorecard."

"My point exactly."

* * *

An hour later, as Phelps pushed a cart through the grocery store aisles, everything looked like something to be eaten competitively. Cereal, baked beans, zucchini, onions, smoked turkey.

Standing at the deli counter while the clerk sliced him a half-pound of low-fat cheese, Phelps remembered his father's love of cheap sandwich meat—liver pudding, olive loaf, head cheese. And Spam, that staple you unwound with a key implanted on the top of the can. Phelps had fried Spam when he was a teenager, coating the meat with brown sugar, and he'd liked it for a few years until he'd left home for college and never eaten another bite of any meat formed by pressing together bits and pieces of scraps and fat and extenders.

His father had told him once that the world ate one hundred million cans of Spam each year. "Three per second," he'd said. "Think of it, Lenny," eating it straight from the can, the jelly it was packed in quivering on thick slices of rye bread, then soaking in as Phelps watched his father stuff the sandwich into his mouth. Somewhere, Phelps was sure, someone was busy training for a Spam race, conditioning himself against the gag reflex for congealed fat.

Sunday afternoon Phelps counted eleven contestants lined up for the doughnut contest. Though each tray held a dozen doughnuts, high school girls in Donut City hats stood behind each contestant to count. A crowd formed, larger than the one he'd stood among for the country band that had been on stage an hour before. Phelps waved at Drew from the fifth row. He felt weak from not eating. Not one thing at the fair was acceptable to his diet. All he'd had was the healthy heart trail mix he carried. There were men years older than him carrying grease-stained paper containers of French fries and chicken fingers. Though most of them were heavy, bellies swelling their shirts, no one looked to have heart problems. But surely they would soon, he thought, not comforted.

The crowd pressed forward as the contestants began to eat. His son folded the doughnuts and stuffed them in his mouth one at a time, sipping water between each one. It looked as if Drew were working them down his throat like large pills.

Eight minutes later, Drew had finished fourth, just completing his second dozen. The winner had eaten thirty-four doughnuts, a guy who looked exactly like the fat ass Phelps had anticipated. Four of the contestants hadn't finished their first dozen; two of them, the youngest, had thrown up. "That's a sorry, sad state of affairs, those boys puking like that on a dozen doughnuts," one of the French-fry eaters, standing just behind Phelps, said.

Though he'd missed out on the win-place-or-show prizes, Drew seemed pleased as they walked among the game booths. "You thought I was lying when I said I could eat two dozen," he said, smiling.

"I thought you were making a foolish guess. There was no way for you to know."

"Except that obvious way."

"You practiced?"

"I trained. I didn't want to be embarrassed."

Drew had to leave for work, but Phelps wandered past the cattle barns and the sheep stalls, holding a beer in a plastic cup and marveling at the size of the hogs. The food, when he re-emerged onto the midway, smelled wonderful. Sausage and onions, lamb kabobs, barbecued ribs. All that dripping fat. It was like seeing the girls in his classes. Even the ordinary looking ones, at eighteen and nineteen, made him ache with desire. His wife had left after Drew had graduated from high school, fifteen years now.

"I never expected the house I lived in to be this quiet," she'd said. "It's like a tomb in here. That's what my mother used to say when my father sat there like a lump. 'It's like a tomb in here.' And he'd just go on with sitting there."

"Quiet doesn't mean unhappy," Phelps had said.

"What's it mean, Len? Mysterious? Are you a man of mystery after all these years?"

"Maybe that's the case," he'd said, the words sounding pathetic, like somebody else had said them, somebody who Phelps loathed.

His wife had softened then. She didn't dislike him; she was just lonely. "Isn't it funny," she'd said, "how you can wake up one morning and know things will never change?"

"You'd be wrong about that," Phelps had said. "That's impossible."

"That's the funny part, Len. It's impossible, but it's happened."

* * *

After Phelps left the fair, exhausted from standing in the sun and walking and drinking three beers, he felt old. The only person he'd ever heard say that was his mother, though she had died younger than his father, at fifty-two. She had been in her forties talking like that, and he'd been young enough to believe that she was right, that forty-seven or forty-eight was so old that of course she was creaky and tired, that his father, two years older, must feel worse but wouldn't admit it.

Now he knew what it was. Sure, there was stiffness, some part of him never quite without pain, but it was more about feeling weak, as if the strength of his muscles were diminishing. Sometimes, lying in bed in the morning, his legs felt so weak that he imagined not being able to walk.

Old, he would think. My legs feel old, and it would take a few minutes of walking in order to smother that thinking for another day, something that led him to believe it wasn't as simple as becoming old. It was worse, something not physical that he didn't want to name.

Food might help, he thought, and he pulled into the same restaurant where he'd watched Drew drink water through a straw. He wanted a fat, greasy sausage smothered in onions, but he sorted through each section of the enormous menu to find the items marked with a bright red valentine. *Healthy heart items*, a key said at the bottom of the first page. There were low-carb items, low-sugar items, low-salt items—half the meals on the menu seemed designed to extend his life, and every one of them made him think how his father would have said, "What's wrong with this place?"

Once, when he was nine, Phelps had set out to meet his father as he drove home from work. His father took the same route every day; he arrived home at the same time. What a surprise it would be for his father to see Phelps walking toward him along the shoulder.

For the first five minutes Phelps was excited. Every approaching car could be his father. When he'd walked for ten minutes, the neighborhood turned unfamiliar, and he began to worry that something had happened to his father.

He walked for another ten minutes—a mile, maybe, he thought—and it was beginning to get dark. He stopped and waited for another minute, hoping, and then he crossed the road and began walking back. Five minutes later, in the twilight, he saw his father's car pass. He waved and began to run, but the car didn't slow.

It was nearly dark when he reached his street. "We've been waiting," his mother said. He sat down without speaking. "What were you doing out there so late? You know your father expects to sit down to supper when he gets home."

They were having fried chicken. His father had wiped a slice of bread through the grease in the bottom of the pan his mother used to cook the chicken. He remembered how the bread glistened, how his mother said, "Oh Glenn," like she was chiding a boy, before she laughed and turned to him, "Now don't you go getting ideas, young man."

The waitress stood poised by the table. She was in her early twenties, he thought, but there were creases of fat in her midsection. His beer was half full, but he pointed to it and croaked, "Could you bring me another of these first?" and she nodded. As soon as she disappeared, he drained the beer, put a five dollar bill on the table and left. The fourteen-ounce draft was $1.75. She wouldn't be disappointed.

Phelps opened a fresh beer when he got home. He carried the rest of the six pack downstairs to save on walking and settled down to watch the Pirates. Given a choice, he'd want to wake up dead. Who wouldn't want to die in his sleep? All that grease and egg yellows and heavy cream being merciful in the end.

* * *

In the morning, he noticed the answering machine's flashing light. Aunt Harriet again. "Uncle Jack decided not to have surgery," she said. "He was too frightened. He said he'd rather have a thousand small fears than one big terror. I thought you'd want to know."

Phelps walked outside with the phone, intending to call her, but he carried it into the back yard without punching in the numbers and stopped on the lawn to look up at the window to his son's old room. When Drew was young, he'd stand on a small, wooden chair to look out, and Phelps had worried so much, he'd taken the chair away. He didn't want to watch in horror as his four-year-old waved and then tumbled through glass.

Drew had cried, but he'd never seen him in the window again. Years later, though, Phelps thought Drew watched him from the window, standing back without the light on so Phelps couldn't see. The thought made him aware of how he looked as he cut the grass or pulled weeds or trimmed the hedges.

Now, holding the phone in the yard, Phelps felt watched. Like a ghost movie, he said to himself, and the banality of it made him walk upstairs and open the door to the empty room.

He was breathing heavily from the climb, but he walked directly to the window, surprised at how low it was. By the time Drew was six or seven years old, he would have been able to see out without the chair. The yard looked unattractive, almost ugly, compared to his neighbors' on either side. A Chemlawn truck came once a month and sprayed their lawns; a truck labeled *landscaping* was regularly parked on the street. Their shrubbery matched. It was evenly trimmed. The flowers were coordinated so that something, from April to October, was always in bloom. In his yard, nothing bloomed after early July, and crabgrass flourished from midsummer on. What had his son thought looking down on him working in a yard so inferior?

When he leaned down to see directly beneath him, Phelps thought he heard footsteps, and he hunched down, gripping the sill with his free hand. He stooped like that for a second or two, then knelt, and finally turned and allowed himself to sit with his back to the wall, staring at the open door.

"Hey," his son's voice called from the bottom of the stairs, "are you up there?"

"Yes," he said, struggling to his feet before Drew could catch him sitting like a sick or lonely man.

In the kitchen Drew glanced at the recycling basket full of beer cans. "Big night?" he said. Phelps regretted not putting them in the garage as soon as he got out of bed.

"I didn't expect you," he said.

"It's OK, Dad," Drew said. "It's not porn."

Drew had brought a dozen doughnuts, all of them slathered in chocolate icing. "Hair of the dog," he said, lifting one of them out and stuffing it in his mouth. He ate them steadily, with a glass of milk. Like a drinker, Phelps thought, like someone who won't stop until all of them are gone. Someone who might eat fifteen or eighteen if he'd brought them home with him.

"You should get over it, Dad," Drew said. "There's no big deal to people getting paid for eating. It's no different than poker."

"You don't kill yourself playing poker."

"That's what you think. Anyway, I rode the bike this morning. I earned these doughnuts. Go ahead and have one. I ordered two custard-filled. I know you love them."

"No thanks."

Drew studied him. "Go ahead," he said. "You know you want to say it."

"What's that?"

"Just get it out. I'm not going to do the work for you."

"You'll grow out of this if you don't kill yourself," Phelps said.

"You did and now you're happy?"

His son sounded like a child, Phelps thought. Like a boy of six or seven asking about his father's divorce. "I'm not killing myself," he said.

"That's what you think."

Drew folded a doughnut and jammed it into his mouth. His cheeks bulged for a few seconds, and then his jaw worked and he swallowed. "They practically melt if you get them wet," he said. "There's nothing to them."

He could eat those two custard ones, Phelps thought. He could help. Instead, he said, "It's your funeral," and walked into his bedroom and started working a crossword puzzle in the book he kept beside the bed. It's what he did to bring on sleep or when a plane he was on began taxiing just prior to take off. He would fill in words in that puzzle in the magazine from the seat pocket until the plane had leveled off.

Once, he'd discovered that the puzzle was already finished in the magazines in the two seats he could reach. One was done in pencil, and he began to trace the letters in with pen, reading each clue before he went over the correct answer, completing the puzzle from top left to bottom right as the plane accelerated.

There had never been a puzzle he couldn't finish, so it wasn't as if he were cheating. And there was the chance the person had entered wrong answers, enough corrections to give him some satisfaction. Until he'd finished, he wouldn't know for certain.

The clue for One Across had been "slang for ecstatic," and he'd traced *giddy* over the penciled letters. At the time, he remembered, he'd wished the puzzle were harder so there were more blank spaces, a clue like "archaic word for dizzy" because he knew the word was *turngiddy*.

There was a tree—a weeping cherry—that he had planted on his son's fourth birthday. "I waited until now so you will remember this when you're old," he explained.

Drew had touched the trunk of the tree as it sat on its root ball while Phelps dug the hole. The tree was nearly four feet high. "The tree is four years old just like you. It's just moving here." Phelps had wanted to believe that, the possibility that the tree had been a seedling that September when his son was born. He hadn't asked at the nursery.

Drew had stuck his thumb over the end of the hose like Phelps had shown him and sprayed water over the leaves and the trunk and the newly turned soil until it turned dark with promise. By the time Phelps had coiled the hose and looped it over the stand at the faucet, his son was walking around the tree, spinning at the same time.

"Like a planet," Phelps had thought, and when Drew, during his fourth orbit, threw his hands up and fell, laughing, he remembered the rare old word he'd discovered once—*turngiddy*—the joy of dizziness.

He thought of telling that story to Drew again, walking outside with him to stand beside the weeping cherry that still drooped in front of the house, but as he walked into the kitchen, he heard pool balls being racked in the basement. All of the doughnuts were gone. He tossed the box into the wastebasket and went downstairs. "Good," Drew said. "Go ahead and break."

Five minutes later, the table nearly empty, Drew cut the eight ball perfectly, and it slid slowly along the rail until it drifted slightly away, curling just enough to hang on the lip of the pocket. Drew didn't wait for Phelps to tap it in. He lifted the ball and placed it an inch from the opposite rail, tapped it with his cue and watched as the eight ball turned inward until it hugged the rail a foot from the pocket. "It's hardly off," Phelps said. "You didn't even notice except for that one shot that happens once every twenty games."

Drew was already at the shelf where the chalk and brush were kept. "Those little wedges the pool table guy left years ago are there someplace," Phelps said, "but the table's too heavy."

"No, it's not."

"You'll hurt your back."

"How can you play on this?" Drew handed him four small wedges. "Slide one under here when I lift."

Phelps knelt and waited, keeping himself from saying, "Be careful." The table leg rose slightly, and he slid the wedge into place.

"Now down here," his son said, moving to the other end.

A moment later the other wedge was inserted, and Drew picked up his cue. Phelps thought the ball rolled true, but Drew looked dissatisfied and rolled it again and then a third time. "You should call that guy who re-felted the table and bitch at him." Drew tapped the ball again, and Phelps held his breath. "That's as good as we can get it with this equipment, but that jackass has a way to make it absolutely perfect."

For the next two games, every shot held its line, but Drew seemed distracted, and before Phelps could rack the balls for a fourth game, he laid his stick back into the brace that hung from the wall. "I'm doing a double shift," he said. "Freeing up a day for later in the summer."

"From 2 p.m. to 6 a.m.? Did you even sleep before you came over?"

"A couple of hours, and yeah, it sucks, but look at it outside. The guy I'm trading double-shifts with is going to be pissed because he was all about going to the shore."

Phelps hadn't noticed the sky going gray. When he went to the window he saw that the patio, nearly at eye level from the basement, was damp even though it didn't seem to be raining. There was a mist in the air, a chill he could feel slipping in through the open window. "A Nor'easter," he said. "This will get worse." He could see the base of the weeping cherry. The grass underneath it glistened.

"Whatever you call it, it's like sixty degrees and wet. He'll be sitting inside somewhere wishing he'd picked another day."

"I looked up all those food records," Phelps said. "They're amazing. Sweet potato casserole. Tiramisu."

Drew smiled and laid the wooden rack on the shelf beside half a dozen worn out chalks. "Did you see the record for mayonnaise?" he said. "One hundred and twenty-eight ounces in eight minutes."

"That's impossible," Phelps said.

"I guess not," Drew said, and then he was up the stairs and gone before Phelps could bring up the record he'd memorized, the one for cow brains, fifty-seven of them in fifteen minutes.

What surprised Phelps was how much those fifty-seven brains weighed. 17.7 pounds, according to the record book. It seemed as if there would be more to a brain than the five ounces he calculated in his head. Cows were enormous, their heads way bigger than a human's.

You can look this up, Phelps thought, and he did. A cow's brain weighed 500 grams; a human's weighed 1500 grams. 500 grams was just over a pound, Phelps remembered. Did water weight cook off? Were those brains somehow trimmed? He followed the table of brain weights to where it listed brains as a percent of body weight. A human's is two percent, maybe a bit more; that cow's brain is a tenth of a percent of its body weight. Phelps thought those numbers made a kind of sense about intelligence until he noticed, farther down the page, that a mouse's brain was more than 3 percent of its body weight.

There seemed to be no measuring how much good brain size did people. It didn't have anything to do, Phelps thought, with his son's

IQ of 160. Three times Drew had been measured, and there those scores were in his high school permanent record. It was astonishing when Phelps thought of it, how the things that puzzle others came easily to his son. How he total-recalled everything.

Phelps remembered his father explaining that fish was brain food. How his father had loved it batter coated and deep fried, telling him to "get smart" when he passed a plate of glistening fish to him. Phelps had never seen Drew eat fish since he'd left home fifteen years ago. *Brain food*—Phelps knew there were people who ate the brains of humans for reasons other than a world's record. To steal that person's strength, for one.

Phelps wished he'd eaten those custard doughnuts. He was so starved his appetite felt like the one he used to have when he was drinking and he stuffed himself with bar food, those little things, salted or spiced, he reached for with his fingers. He could eat chips or popcorn or peanuts nonstop.

Finest Pizza had set up a table of its items for an all-you-can-eat Monday lunch buffet. Five kinds of pizza, cinnamon sticks, stromboli, cheese bread. Phelps looked at the clock. The buffet would be up for another fifty minutes. Five and a half pounds, the buffet record holder had eaten in twelve minutes, but Phelps decided to take his time. If he couldn't manage that weight, he could come back next Monday and finish. He would ask the waiter how much a pizza weighed, how heavy the stromboli was. Phelps was sure the franchise knew these things. All he had to do was ask.

THE BLAZER SESTINA

PAUL'S MOTHER DIED at 2 p.m. the afternoon of November 22, 1963. "Kennedy died before her," my mother said, while she listened to Walter Cronkite announce the time of his death. "It doesn't matter what Cronkite says," she went on. "Kennedy was a Catholic, so they pretended he wasn't dead until a priest could give him the last rites."

Paul's mother wasn't Catholic. She wasn't anything, as far as I'd ever heard her say, which made her the only mother I knew who didn't go to church. She would have sent a priest away. She would have told him to mind his own business if she hadn't had something blow up inside her head.

"I have such a headache," she'd said, according to Paul, and then she'd stood up, taken two steps and fallen flat on the floor of the kitchen where she'd been eating toasted cheese sandwiches with Paul because he'd stayed home sick from school to miss our American history test.

"An aneurysm," Paul's stepfather said.

"His real father wouldn't even have noticed she was dead," my mother said. "By two o'clock Tom Sherba would have been drunk. What a shame, and him living only five miles away, not even decent enough to fade into the sunset after he ended it with her by not taking care of himself." My mother kept watching the six o'clock news while she talked. "And Lyndon Johnson—my God," she said. "We're in for it now. Just look at him, like something the cat dragged in."

I thought Lyndon Johnson looked sad and old. He looked like somebody who could die without being shot in the head.

* * *

Saturday morning our high school team had an intersquad scrimmage scheduled, and nobody was absent except Paul. Our first game was Friday, the day after Thanksgiving, and this scrimmage was supposed to help Coach Rodman decide who was starting and what order he'd use to substitute. Without Paul at practice, I got moved to backup center and had to guard Jim Vail, who was four inches taller than me and a sure thing to start. Playing out of position like that, I knew I wasn't a candidate for first forward off the bench, that Coach Rodman had me penciled in for garbage time because Jim Vail was going to chew me up while two other guys sweated it out to see who would play while the game was in doubt.

I pushed and shoved Jim Vail until he swung his elbows after he came down with a rebound. One sharp elbow scraped under my chin like a prehistoric razor, and I backed off next time down the floor, Jim Vail taking a pass so close to the hoop his jump hook left his hand a foot from the rim.

"Think yourself big," Coach Rodman shouted at me. "Winning's a choice, not a chance." I plodded along. I pretended I was setting up outside to draw Jim Vail away from the basket, but without a position at stake, my goal was to get off the floor with my jaw intact. "Obstacles are opportunities," Coach Rodman hollered as I clanked a twenty-foot jump shot off the back of the rim, but I stayed outside. Thanksgiving was coming; there was turkey to eat. Unless somebody sprained an ankle or broke a leg, I wasn't going to play unless we were more than twenty points behind or ahead.

So I was happy when, an hour after we started, Coach Rodman called practice off. "Everything's half-assed," he said. "This Kennedy thing. Paul's mother. And everything comes in threes. Next thing you know one of you will break his neck."

The name Jim Vail popped right up for me, but I trotted to the locker room with my head down as if I were as disappointed as one of the starting five. By the time I'd showered and dressed I'd decided Coach Rodman had made up his mind about this team the week before when he'd posted the cut list and six guys had cleaned out their lockers while the rest of us jogged upstairs to run our fifteen laps.

My mother, when I got home, was enraged. "I didn't know where you were when I came back from the grocery store," she said. "I never thought you'd have practice. What kind of man keeps you for even one minute at a time like this?"

"He let us out early."

"I'm surprised he didn't have poor Paul Sherba playing." She was walking around the house, synchronizing the clocks while she talked, and I had to follow her into every room but my bedroom and the bathroom.

"He couldn't. Paul was absent yesterday so he's not allowed. And he hasn't been Paul Sherba for three years."

My mother heaved a sigh. "Yes, he has," she said. "He's been Paul Sherba his whole life."

* * *

I walked the two blocks to Paul's house after lunch. His stepfather was still at the funeral home getting things arranged for the first visiting hours at three o'clock. "Ogrodnik's," Paul said. "You know."

I knew, all right, my father had been laid out there after his accident at the packing plant two years before. Paul's voice sounded scratchy and low like he'd been smoking all morning. There was a half empty quart bottle of Blue Ribbon on the floor by the couch, and when Paul passed it my way, I gave him a question-mark look before I took a long swallow. "He'll lose count," Paul said, reading my mind. "People are bringing food and stuff. The fridge is so crowded he won't know one's missing. You can pitch it over the hill behind Kramer's on your way home."

I nodded, but I wasn't so sure. Paul's stepfather, Mr. Koch, was a guy who counted everything. And he was a guy who kept half-finished beer in the refrigerator in the quart bottles he bought to save a few pennies. Blue Ribbon—he unscrewed the caps and poured a glass and screwed the cap back on as if it were milk.

When Paul's real father heard about that, the three of us watching *Bonanza* and drinking Iron City from cans in his living room, he told us, "A man who leaves beer in a bottle for the next day is nobody I want to talk to." Paul laughed then, but that was in September, when Paul turned sixteen two months after I had, and his real father had just bought a case and told him to celebrate.

* * *

I drove to Ogrodnik's at five o'clock. "Dinner's at six," my mother said, and for once I was glad to say, "OK," because I wanted to have a reason to leave at 5:45. Mr. Wahl, our American History teacher, was just in front of me as I stepped into the short line by the viewing room doorway. He was wearing his dark gray blazer. He'd worn camel yesterday, blue on Thursday, and the dark gray Wednesday, so I knew he'd made an effort at showing sorrow; Mr. Wahl would have worn green or maroon or his light gray if Ogrodnik's was his classroom. He owned six blazers in those colors, rotated them, Paul had told me, like the end words in the lines of a sestina—green, blue, two shades of gray, maroon, camel.

Paul had written a sestina, the kind of thing he did during American history instead of paying attention to Mr. Wahl. He'd shown me how the words went at the end of the lines, but I couldn't keep track. But I understood enough to know Mr. Wahl never wore the same color until he'd run through a six-day cycle.

"You practice today?" Mr. Wahl said to me as we waited to greet Paul's stepfather.

"For an hour," I said.

Mr. Wahl nodded, as if that were a perfect answer. "You could do worse than listening 100 percent to Coach Rodman," he said. "You know what he is, don't you? He's the Dale Carnegie of basketball."

I was glad the line moved up and he was almost next. I didn't want to ask him who Dale Carnegie was, thinking he might have something to do with the Carnegie we'd studied in history, the one we were supposed to revere because he'd paid for the biggest library and museum in Pittsburgh.

"You remember the advice in *Appointment with Success?*"

"Think and grow rich," I said, reciting the slogan on the cover of the book Mr. Wahl read to us every Monday.

Mr. Wahl smiled. "Yes," he said. "And do you remember the eight steps to achievement?"

"Sure," I lied. He'd written them on the blackboard in September and had us copy them every day for a week. "You write something three times or more, you remember it forever," he'd said, but I wasn't going to have to prove him wrong, because I could see the woman in front of him step away.

"Excuse me," he said, and now that I was in the front of the line, I could see Paul sitting behind Mr. Koch, his chair pushed back against the wall beside one where Cheryl McNally, who lived on the block between Paul's house and mine, was sitting. He'd been dating her since school had started, driving her, for the last month, to his real father's apartment as if it were a motel. He had a key and a father who went out almost every night and was never back before midnight unless a woman dragged him. "*Master your moods*," I suddenly thought. "*Do it today*." The first two steps to success. Cheryl McNally was patting Paul's hand and leaning close as they whispered to each other. Even when she sat up as Paul looked my way, she kept her hand resting on Paul's. I thought she looked like somebody's mother sitting like that, but I knew that was one idea I was going to keep to myself.

I gave him a nod before I stepped forward, shook Mr. Koch's hand, and said, "My sympathy," exactly like my mother had instructed before I left.

Mr. Koch pressed his left hand over my right as if he meant to extend our handshake. I waited for him to say something, but he had already turned toward the next guest, a woman from our street, and both his hands dropped away so suddenly I was left reaching into air like a mime pretending to be dragged by a dog on a leash.

I didn't go by the casket. I didn't want to see Paul's mother when she was dead, but I stepped behind Mr. Koch and walked over to Paul. "Blazer Man giving you a pep talk?" Paul said.

Cheryl looked puzzled, but she didn't say anything. "Who's Dale Carnegie?" I said.

Paul smiled. "Who wants to know?"

"Wahl called Coach Rodman the Dale Carnegie of basketball."

"Maybe they'll name the school library after him."

I gave up and waited for Paul to decide what came next. "You do your isometrics at practice?" he said, and I saw his hand slide up and over Cheryl's, then trail along her sleeve as she settled closer to him in her chair.

"Sure, like always." Coach Rodman had us press our hands against each other and push; he had us grip our hands together and pull. We pushed against the wall with our arms and our legs while he counted to ten and told us we only got out of these exercises what we put into them.

"I think Wahl has Charles Atlas confused with Dale Carnegie. Don't you remember Wahl's speech about doing isometrics for the mind?"

I knew who Charles Atlas was. I'd seen his ads for dynamic tension in a thousand comic books. Paul smiled again. "Isometrics. Dynamic tension. It's all the same," Paul said. "Wahl is so sure we don't know anything he thinks we'll be dazzled by a new name for *debate*."

"Communism vs. Democracy," I said, naming one we'd had in October.

"Christianity vs. Atheism," Cheryl piped up, naming the one we'd had last week.

Paul watched Wahl leave. "Isometric of the mind my ass," he said then. "Remember the missile crisis?"

I relaxed. Finally, something had sunk in. The seniors on the basketball team had told us that, the year before, Mr. Wahl had split his classes into "Bomb Cuba" and "Don't Bomb Cuba" for a debate. Every day, after they watched the news on television, they could change their minds and move to the other side of the room. The last day, before Kruschev backed down, there were only two students left on the "Don't Bomb" side. Mr. Wahl had stood in the middle of the room and nodded. "Act, not react," he had said. "The physics of war." The two girls sitting in "Don't Bomb" had begun to cry. "Thank you, students," he had added as the bell rang. "Good luck to all of you."

I wondered what Wahl would have us debate after Thanksgiving. So far this year he hadn't had any crises to inspire him beyond what he said to everybody who did worse than a B on tests he was handing back. "This should show you something," he repeated. "You do your best at everything, not just what you prefer."

"You know if you've been bad or good," Paul said after Mr. Wahl ran through that routine a second time, and then a third. Paul was getting a D in history even though he knew the answers to every history question on *College Bowl*.

"The wonder boy," Mr. Koch would say every time Paul answered a question while we watched with Paul's mother on Sunday afternoons. "Harvard," he started calling him.

As in, "Hey, Harvard, you flunking out of high school?"

I loved watching *College Bowl* with Paul and his mother when Mr. Koch wasn't around. Some weeks he'd win just by himself, outscoring Radcliffe or Cornell or Skidmore. Paul's mother would make popcorn, but Paul only ate during the commercials.

Last Sunday Mr. Koch had poured himself a glass of beer and sat in a chair with the newspaper while we watched. Paul had rung in way before Colgate to answer *villanelle*. He'd nailed the bonus question, saying *pantoum* while Colgate's four students looked at each other and guessed *limerick* as if they'd never been to college at all. Paul's mother had reached over and squeezed his arm. Mr. Koch had looked up from his newspaper and said, "Put that on your application, Harvard."

* * *

When I made it home by 5:55, I asked my mother whether or not she thought Paul's real father would come to the funeral home. "Not likely," she said. "Not with Diane's relatives around. Not unless they all go blind."

My mother poured me a glass of Hawaiian Punch and told me Paul needed two fathers like he needed a hole in the head. She said that about every comic book I'd ever bought, every record, every bottle of soda and fast-food hamburger, but for once I was listening. A hole in the head—Kennedy had one, that was sure, and Paul's mother, too, if you could look inside her skull and find the place where she'd sprung that fatal leak.

Suddenly there was a commotion outside. A man shouting. A door slamming. My mother, standing in front of the stove with a spoon in her hand, looked toward the window, but she didn't move. "I'll take a look," I said.

"Make it quick," she said. "Dinner's practically on the table."

A garbage truck was pulled to the side of the street, two tires up on our next-door neighbor's front lawn. I saw Mr. and Mrs. Meenan rush outside together as if they meant to move that truck, but then I heard voices layered over each other as I stepped across our front yard, two men who must have been in that truck looking down at a man in coveralls lying on the asphalt. "Whipped right off," one of the standing men said, and I knew that the man in coveralls had been standing on the garbage truck, not paying attention to the low telephone wire that crossed the street to the pole in the Meenan's side yard.

"Don't you go being nosy," my mother warned. She was standing in the doorway and looking back at the kitchen as if she expected to see clouds of billowing smoke pouring from the oven, but I pushed through our hedges and heard the downed garbage man softly moaning, which made it seem as if he would be all right as soon as he pulled himself together. It was only if you were quiet that things were serious—the unconscious, the choking—my mother always preached. If you could make a sound, you were still in the world of breath and heartbeat.

But the man didn't switch, finally, to words, beginning to swear or explain where he hurt. His moan, in fact, stayed elementary— unhhhhh, unhhhhh—as if he were humming like my mother said that wire over the street did if you pressed your ear against it.

The ambulance came. Sunday morning, at church, a woman who was a nurse told my mother the garbage man was alive but in a coma. "A skull fracture," she said. "He might snap out of it any minute, but you never know about these things."

* * *

We didn't subscribe to the Sunday newspaper. "All ads," my mother said, "and five times the cost." We never watched television until after lunch, so when I walked back to Paul's to see how things were going before he had to sit at Ogrodnik's at three o'clock, I knew as much about what had happened in the world that morning as the garbage man in a coma.

Paul opened the door, but Mr. Koch was right behind him, look- ing excited. "You see it?" he said.

"See what?" I said, and Paul mumbled "Jesus Christ" loud enough for Mr. Koch to lay his hands on Paul's shoulders.

"Your house doesn't follow the news?" Mr. Koch said, and when I shrugged, the best I could do at, "No," he added, "Somebody shot the bastard who killed Kennedy."

Paul twisted away from his stepfather. "So?" he said, and Mr. Koch flicked his hand out and slapped Paul hard enough to turn his head. "So?" Paul said again, but he sidestepped to keep himself out of reach.

"You're watching history here," Paul's stepfather said. "When you decide to grow up, you'll wonder what the hell you were doing while the world decided who you were going to be."

"I thought it was decided already," Paul said. "I'm Harvard."

I turned as if a set of plaster-of-Paris Amish figures on the windowsill was suddenly important to examine. Paul's mother had collections of culture-by-family. Every windowsill in the living room and dining room had a set. The Amish. Indians. Eskimos. African villagers. Anybody you could paint a costume on for easy identification.

I looked at the Amish father. He was muscular and fit, as if he had never swallowed a beer or sat on a couch eating pizza and potato chips. The Indian father by the next window looked as if he could play tight end for the Steelers. Instead of hearing Paul's stepfather say anything else, I heard the television come on behind me. Kennedy's assassin, a newscaster was saying, was dead. When Paul walked by me and through the door, I tried to watch the footage of Oswald being shot. The clip was short. I watched the whole thing before I followed Paul outside to see what he was up to.

"If somebody shoots Oswald's killer tomorrow, Dad number two will have something to watch before the funeral," Paul said.

I wanted to say something, but every opinion I could think of seemed wrong. "I'm coming to the funeral," I said. "School's called off for Kennedy."

"I should go in there and turn on the Steelers and the Bears," Paul said. "Football isn't called off."

"You do your isometrics this morning?" I said, and Paul laughed.

"Let Jim Vail push a wall. He'll be playing the whole game unless he gets in foul trouble."

Mr. Koch stepped outside and waved Paul to the porch. I watched him start up the stairs, but I didn't turn for home like I ordinarily would have because I saw that Mr. Koch was carrying the baseball-size jagged stone he kept on top of the television. For a second I thought he was going to slap Paul with it, but he was just juggling it from hand to hand, keeping himself busy while Paul slowly climbed the eight steps.

That stone was from Mt. Rushmore. Mr. Koch had stuffed it into the big purse Paul's mother had been carrying and brought it home last summer. Even now, Paul wasn't sure whether it was legal to take stones from the base of the mountain, but Paul's stepfather was proud of that stone. "It's from Lincoln," he said. "It was at the bottom of his side of the mountain."

Watching Mr. Koch juggling that stone, I expected to hear somebody had started a Kennedy head in the side of some mountain. I thought about Kennedy and his splattered brain, how healing the hole in his head had been impossible. Kennedy would be up there on the mountain forever. He'd be enormous.

If somebody asked me, I could tell them Paul's father could carve the model the rock blasters could work from. Even my mother admired the animals he carved from soap. "That Tom Sherba," she'd say. "If only he could keep his hands busy twenty-four hours a day."

Bears, camels, lions, deer. Paul had a zoo in his room from all the soap animals his father had given him. "He tells me to use them up, that he has a thousand more where those came from, but I can't," Paul had told me. "And then every time I see him he gives me another one like he's replacing one that's gone down the drain after twenty showers."

I walked home trying to figure out how you could give a shit about someone and still fuck it up. I thought about how I might, before I recognized it in myself, turn into the kind of person I despised—Mr. Koch, Coach Rodman, Mr. Wahl and his blazer sestina.

* * *

Sunday night I drove Paul to his real father's apartment. Paul was excited, wanting to talk with his father, to hear stories, maybe, about the way his mother had been before he was born, but even as we knocked on the door, I knew things weren't going to work out, because the music from inside was way too loud.

A woman answered. She was holding a drink and wearing a bathrobe that I'd seen Paul's father lounging around in. "Huh?" she said, and then she laughed, glancing back at Paul's father, who looked as if he were trying to find the volume dial on his hi-fi. "This for you?" she yelled over the music.

Paul's father nodded, but he couldn't seem to separate himself from the hi-fi. "My son and his best friend," he said, wobbling.

Paul stepped past the woman, but he didn't approach his father. "How old are you?" the woman said. "You're as skinny as a homo."

Paul's father picked up a drink that he'd set down on an album cover, one hand still fiddling at the dials. He didn't act like he'd heard her.

"That's an absurd analogy," Paul said, sounding like he was giving an answer on *College Bowl.*

"Analowhat?" She turned to Paul's father. "You hear this boy of yours? He sounds like a homo."

The music roared up, and Paul's father walked into the bathroom. It was just instrumental, jazz or something without a melody that I could make out. Nobody turned that kind of music up too loud, but then I heard the sound of vomiting from the bathroom.

"Is this how he gets?" I asked Paul.

"No."

I nodded like I was relieved, but then Paul said, "He never threw up in our house."

The woman, if she'd heard, wasn't letting on. "So," she said, "you two more than friends?" I heard the toilet flush, but Paul's father didn't come out. "So?" the woman said, but she'd lost interest and didn't get any further.

Paul scooped up two soap horses from the coffee table. "Tell my father thanks for the stallions," he said, and then he mounted one on the other. "See?" he said. "They're homos."

* * *

Ogrodnik had a television on in the back room showing Kennedy's funeral. When I peeked in for a minute, I saw the horse with the backwards stirrups, the drums sounding as if we should crowd around and watch—I felt like some kind of asshole, but later I saw Mr. Koch step through that door, and when he didn't come right back out, I started counting, getting to two hundred and seventeen before he backed out, still watching, and then put a handkerchief to his eyes like he'd gotten something under the contact lenses he wore.

After a while, I needed a break from looking solemn, but when I slipped out the side door, I saw Paul's father standing outside of Isaly's, a store half a block away. He was licking an ice cream cone, the tall pyramid scoop kind Isaly's sold. I turned into the alley behind Ogrodnik's and started walking in the other direction.

A half hour later, when I was finished killing time on Etna's back streets, he was still there. And still licking a cone, so he'd gone back inside at least once, maybe to warm up, but also to get another cone. My mother, coming up to me so fast I thought she'd been watching the door, listened as I explained.

"It's what he does to keep from drinking," she said. "You keep an eye out. They've called Diane's family for the last viewing, but I'll bet he'll have another fresh one before the service starts."

I took that to mean I could stay outside until the funeral began. Paul's father was gone, though, when I checked the sidewalk in front of Isaly's. Without him there to see me, I stayed on the side porch, telling myself I'd go back inside exactly three minutes before the service so I didn't have to speak to anybody until after this was over.

Which is why I saw Ogrodnik's back door swing open and Paul's father step out. Ogrodnik held the door with one hand and shook Mr. Sherba's hand with the other, and I understood that he'd allowed Paul's father to see his wife between the last viewing and the beginning of the ceremony. He was the last to see her before Ogrodnik closed the coffin.

When the service began, I looked at Ogrodnik, a man who had buried my father two years ago, though it had been McNeely, a mile from here, who had laid out all four of my grandparents, dead within the last six years. "Heredity," Paul had said to me last winter when my grandfather, the last of them, had died at sixty-two, "is not your friend." Ogrodnik seemed younger than sixty-two, though I had so little experience with the ordinary health of old age he might as well have been seventy.

Ogrodnik moved as fluidly as Mr. Koch, who still ran for twenty-five minutes each evening before dinner. "Twenty-five minutes is what the heart needs to make a difference," he'd told me more than once. "People fool themselves with fifteen or twenty minutes. They'll live to regret it."

"Or die," I'd said the second time he told me, but Mr. Koch didn't laugh or even change expression, and as far as Paul and heredity were concerned, my father's death was by machine, and Paul had just received, despite all of his grandparents being alive, something to consider about his gene pool, a mother dead at forty-one, a father who seemed to carry the genes for bad habits and self-destruction.

How long had Ogrodnik given Paul's father alone with his dead wife? Two minutes? Ogrodnik, nervous perhaps, might have busied himself with rearranging chairs while he listened for footsteps approaching the closed door.

The service droned on. Paul's stepfather had invited the minister from the Lutheran church he went to. After he started talking, you could tell he didn't know anything about Paul's mother. "She was a wonderful mother," he said. "A hard-working woman." I saw Paul clenching and unclenching his fists. Cheryl McNally had disappeared. The minister hesitated as if he were trying to recall something important. "She brought out the best in those who knew her," he said, getting started again.

My mother was right. Paul's father was holding another cone when we walked outside. I saw Paul looking at him as he shuffled behind the coffin. I thought of Paul's father breathing on the face of his wife as he leaned to look closely at her, perhaps even kiss her, the smell of sugar mixed, I was certain, with bourbon. And then, when the coffin slid into the hearse, I saw Paul's father pitch that cone into the street and hurry to his car.

* * *

Paul called me at eight o'clock. He sounded drunk, and he wanted me to come over because his stepfather had told him to take care of himself because he wouldn't be home until late. I promised my mother I'd be home by ten o'clock. "There's school, you know," she said. "Kennedy's in the ground now."

Nobody was in the living room or kitchen, so I climbed the stairs.

The first thing I saw when I walked into Paul's bedroom was Cheryl McNally holding a quart of Blue Ribbon and mouthing the words to a song The Skyliners were singing through the speakers of Paul's record player. "Close your eyes," she lip-synched, "take a deep breath—ahhhhh." She exhaled so long and so hard I thought she was deflating, but she recovered, whispering, "Open your heart," toward Paul before she took a sip of beer.

"I love these old songs," she said to me. "Don't you?" She held out the beer to me. "Here," she said. "Enjoy. I've had enough." She took Paul's hands and pulled them around her, beginning to dance, her mouth pressed against his ear.

I took the beer and walked back downstairs. I heard the Fleetwoods begin to sing from Paul's room, and I settled down in front of the television wishing for some sadness to transform me into someone girls wanted to give themselves to. Almost all of the stations had Kennedy stories, but two had patriotic movies, and I settled on James Cagney in *Yankee Doodle Dandy*. It was all the way to the part, during World War I, when Cagney sings and dances to "Over There." I figured an hour and Paul would reappear. What did Paul want me here for? Cheryl McNally had a father who was already checking his watch against the clock in his kitchen. She lived six houses away, close enough to walk home, close enough for Mr. McNally, if he figured she was here, to walk upstairs and pound Paul with his fists.

Twenty minutes later, I heard Cheryl shout, "Hey you down there."

Cagney was shuffling and tapping, and I waited, counting to eight before she shouted again and I started upstairs.

Paul was sitting on the floor beside his bed, his head resting against the mattress. Propped on one elbow on the bed, Cheryl was watching Paul arrange what looked like fifty soap animals. The album they'd been listening to was spinning with the needle tracing the same circle near the hole in the center. Thk, thk, thk, it was whispering in the style The Fleetwoods used. Paul's mother had played that record a thousand times. "Come Softly to Me." "Mr. Blue." I remembered there were two girls and one guy in the group, but now they were as quiet as the television at Ogrodnik's, the volume turned off because he was being paid to take care of the funeral in Etna, not the one in Washington, DC.

Paul looked like Noah sorting things out. Cheryl was wearing Paul's shirt and nothing else, something I knew for certain because it was unbuttoned. "You know what Dad number two told me?" Paul said, holding a bear in each hand. I shook my head. "He said he was proud of me for being as brave as John-John at his Daddy's funeral."

I felt like my tongue was swollen, that I'd choke if it moved. Paul placed the bears beside what looked to be a wolf but might have been a dog. "He said he felt like Jackie when he was standing beside Mom's grave. What the fuck?"

I imagined myself kneeling on the floor with Paul and walking some of his animals to the door and down the stairs, staying on all fours as I worked them toward the kitchen where they could wait on the table beside the leftover pizza I'd seen there. I'd sit and wait for Paul to creep through the door, pushing a couple of dogs to a chair where he'd leave them so they could stare up at the rabbit and the cat so far out of reach.

Paul didn't look up, but he started telling the story of how his mother had died. He got to the headache part, and Cheryl began to twist one of the buttons in the middle of the shirt, pulling it farther apart so both her breasts were exposed. "And then she fell," Paul said, still staring at the bears as if he expected them to move. He was reciting as if he'd memorized this story by repeating it three times or more. "Never become discouraged," I caught myself thinking, the phrase clawing its way up from *Appointment with Success*, and I wanted to bash my head with Mr. Koch's Lincoln rock to keep from remembering anymore of those eight steps.

Cheryl rubbed that button across her breasts then, back and forth, and I understood she wasn't nervous with Paul's story—she was impatient. I thought if I walked toward her she would shrug herself out of that shirt and lift her arms to receive me while Paul, in his story, called for an ambulance and began to cry.

THE PROMISES OF LABELS

SIX WEEKS ISN'T LONG unless every one of those forty-two days is a space between you and what you love most, and for Rick Morton, it was the Westberg Hotel, from which he'd been banished for fighting.

The rules were written on signs that were tacked on each of the walls so nobody who'd been in the bar for more than five minutes had an excuse for saying he didn't know. FIGHTING: First offense—six weeks; Second offense—life.

There were those who were forever banished, having to make do with the Royalty, the one other bar in Westberg, itself someplace that didn't attract fighters in the first place, meaning it lacked spirit somehow, and those with a lifetime banishment drifted in and out, but never settled, because there was a preponderance of placid faces and benign dispositions, no tension in that bar except what was within them. Fourteen years, for a fact, Morton had been drinking at the Westberg, and not once had he set foot inside the Royalty, relying on years of hearsay he trusted more than a minister's sermon.

So when Rick Morton inspected the Royalty three times during the first weeks of the lockout, each visit filled him with dread and reminded him to take stock of himself. He needed discipline or he needed to move to another town, because drinking in the Royalty was like drinking in church.

* * *

Life without parole—you had to give some thought and consideration to just what would cause you to give up your place in the world of pleasure. Some unforgivable grievance. Some intolerable words or gestures. Rick Morton wondered plenty about just what they might be so he would know his priorities when his six weeks were up at twelve o'clock midnight, August 17th, not one second sooner or later, and he would walk in to cheers and a draft being poured on-the-house so it slid across the bar exactly at the moment he settled onto a stool.

When he thought about it, he knew it was discovering that a chronic asshole could spike a jagged surge of rage within him that fucked up everything, the recognition that there were people, some within the same room, he suddenly couldn't abide. Thus his fight with Joe Gerber, a boy really, twenty-two but looking as if that were his age only on a fake ID, a guy who got laid in order to tell people he did.

What started things that night was Gerber loudly declaring, "Sounds like somebody's humping over there."

Morton had looked, of course, just like everybody else in the Westberg. The woman in question was Callie Wertz, who had a way of stifling a laugh, like some people stifle sneezes, embarrassed, the pitch of unnnnnhh rising, then collapsing into a short audible breath. He knew Callie, a daughter to Wade Wertz, the oldest guy he worked with at Builders Paradise and someone who never set foot in the Westberg or the Royalty, and Gerber's tone and volume didn't sit well with him. Though it was true she was straddling Wayne Kratzer's lap, bringing up the physical possibility, all he seemed to be doing was whispering something in her ear that made her press her lips together.

"This here bitch of mine squeals better than that from just my finger," Gerber said.

Morton had looked at the girl beside Gerber then. On the weak side of ordinary looking, he thought. Younger than Gerber, probably underage, she'd pulled her chair around beside him at a table, the two of them sitting in front of the jukebox like the first fans at a rock show pressed against the stage. What a world, he'd thought, that accounted for her hooked up with such a shithead, but the girl didn't change expression. She looked like somebody who was willing to listen to Joe Gerber talk in exchange for not having to stay home or drink with girls two years out of high school who were getting anxious about their lot in life.

"Let it be," was all Morton had said. After two hours at the bar and a day of standing on his feet among items he hoped never to buy himself, he was tired of anything that sniffed of arrogance.

"You a teacher or something?" Gerber had said. "You think this is homeroom?"

Morton had shrugged, but there was no question he'd started a snowball down a long hill. Callie brushed her hand in front of her face as if she were erasing a blackboard. Kratzer shook his head. "That your sister over there squealing?" Gerber said. "You jealous?"

He stared at the girl beside Gerber, deciding whether or not he might be saving her from something, and then he finished his beer, knowing it was his last in the Westberg for six weeks. Joe Gerber wasn't going to stop; it was just a question of what he was going to say next, which happened to be, "Funny you should be jealous, cause you look like a dick sucker to me."

Callie, he noticed, was standing now, and he wondered briefly if she were making room for Kratzer to get to his feet. "One of us has to leave," Morton said, trying one more hopeless line.

"I ain't going nowhere, so go jerk your own self off outside. I got my own sweet pussy."

He had to admit Joe Gerber had thumped him a few good ones, but he'd broken Gerber's nose for him and cracked a few ribs with the toe of his boot. He'd never kicked a man before, but Gerber seemed like the right guy to start with, and he didn't regret it. He'd even thought how a man might take to a knife or a gun when dealing with Joe Gerber, provoked past caring about anything but doing harm.

* * *

One effect of banishment was work seemed shorter because he wasn't watching the clock so hard at Builders Paradise, where his shift ended at 6 p.m. It was one of those warehouse "palaces," the idea of discounts plugged into shoppers' brains by the size of the building. Such obvious volume had to mean cheaper, though Morton couldn't exactly say whether this was true because he didn't have household projects, what with always living in apartments.

"The Hangar," all the employees called it, and it was never quite comfortable because you could feel the cold at your feet year round, no foundation under the polished cement floor, a surface that guaranteed, all the women employees said, a matched pair of varicose-veined legs by fifty.

What he'd learned in the three years he'd worked at Builders Paradise was there were two categories of customers, the first of which was the handyman/survivalist kind who inspected every board in a volume purchase as if he could detect the tiniest flaws. That kind spoke in a jargon of home repair that he interpreted as testing him, though he understood that quality was proportional to price, the fundamental ratio of any business, and he stuck to it. "You'll get better wear from this," he said, speaking beside an assortment of bathroom fixtures. "It's a few dollars more, but it's worth it."

The handymen would frown as if nothing could be that simple. But the rest were worse, because the second kind were inept and helpless, men driven to the store by necessity and wives. Men who wandered the aisles as if they were at a video store, waiting for something that looked familiar to catch their eye until, finally despairing, they asked him about the differences among three kinds of driveway sealer, whether the cracks that spider-webbed through the asphalt from the roots of a tree they'd planted ten years ago and were surprised had gotten so large could be filled by using the "heavy duty."

Or four kinds of deck sealer, whether it really lasted two years or three or even four, as guaranteed. They wanted to know if the promises of labels would be kept, and Morton always subtracted a year from every pledge, and two or even five years from the longer vows. "I recommend two years," he said, for the three-year guarantees. "You can count on ten-to-twelve, for sure," he said, when the label declared fifteen years of maintenance-free service. The novices would nod and thank him, carrying cans of material they dreaded opening, tasks they'd slog through thinking about the beer or television or both that waited for them at the end. None of them would ever save receipts or return the forms that established the guarantees. If a space heater broke, they'd curse and buy a new one. If it malfunctioned in a way that produced carbon monoxide, they'd be found dead in their bedrooms.

Ron and Jake Dixon, brothers near his age who were his best

friends from work, seemed to know more than he did. Both of them had built their own decks, shaping and fitting boards until they produced what to Morton were miracles of carpentry. Ron had even put in a brick patio that looked like the one pictured in the Builders Paradise brochure. What Morton had was an apartment that kept his ignorance a secret, because all he had to do was change kitty litter and carry a bag of the garbage that stunk to the end of the driveway every Tuesday evening.

* * *

The first night he visited the Royalty, the bar was so empty Morton turned self-conscious and stayed, as if his father were sitting beside him, nearly sober. The place, he decided, looked so much like a church basement social hall that a bingo game could have begun without him being surprised.

For starters, it didn't have a jukebox. The music was piped in like it was in a grocery store, but almost at once he knew it was a radio station, classic soft rock, and after he heard a set of commercials followed by Elton John, Fleetwood Mac, and The Eagles, he stopped hearing it.

And there weren't any pictures on the walls, which were painted beige, helping to maintain the uniform light throughout the room. There wasn't a pool table, and the bar was half the length of the one at the Westberg, just eight stools, so that nearly all of the crowd, if the place were full, would be sitting at tables like families.

Yet at 10 p.m. there were just five seats taken at the bar—a group of three middle-aged guys clustered near the television watching the Headline News Channel and two solos who'd set up away from the television with a stool between them. Morton sat in the middle, choosing a seat beside the younger of the solos, a guy he guessed to be around fifty, Wade Wertz's age. "Stranger in town," the man said without inflection.

"Not hardly. Just in here."

The man examined his face as if he was trying to place him. "You engage in fisticuffs up yonder?" he said.

"You nailed it."

The man tapped his half empty mug against Morton's fresh one and nodded. "Welcome to that club."

"I've never seen you before."

"It's running up to twenty years now since I set foot in there."

"A two-timer?"

The man snorted and drank. "There's plenty nights I'm put out from wanting to fight with some horse's ass, but I know where I want to be. That first offense was permanent. You look me up for 1985. You'll see."

Morton was ready to let it go, but the man kept on. "Just that there once. Never went back. Thought I would, but then with the six weeks and all, I fell out of the habit. It can happen. There's more like me comes in here. Most nights I don't even bother with this. A beer's just as good and twice as cheap in front of the television. You married?"

"No."

"You should put this time to good use. I met my little woman in here." He swept his mug around in a half circle that brought the beer close to spilling, and Morton counted eight women, four in a group and four in pairs. Under forty and over forty, he guessed, but those younger women looked like versions of female Builders Paradise employees, a little too thick, a little frumpy, women who had grown comfortable not being noticed by men.

"That's nice," he said.

"Mind you, she don't set foot in here nowadays these ten years or more. 'Enough's enough' is her motto, but look here now, you tell me what your prize fight was all about."

"Just a jackass I couldn't truck with."

"He have a name?"

"Gerber."

The man nodded. "I know his kind and him to boot. I seen him a week back when you must have been fresh out of the Westberg. He was busted up some."

"Some."

"That Gerber fellow's not the worst I've seen in here. There's them that hits their women for a fact. They keep it to themselves, the ones that do physical harm. Far's I know Gerber's just talk. For now, at least. Elstwise, the word would spread like it does."

Morton examined the other solo and the three news-headline watchers. None of them looked as if they'd raise a hand, even if provoked. "Before I made that call, I'd want to know the truth of such word-of-mouth," he said.

"Verifying's hard, I'll give you that," the man said. "But you can't be a vigilante for what's said. That's work for God."

* * *

Three days later, during the second night he spent in the Royalty, Morton bought a robot cat from a guy at the bar who, declaring he'd unload it for the best offer, set it off along the floor. The thing walked like a cat and sounded like a cat. "The wife hates this," the man said. "It reminds her of her allergies. She says she starts to get short of breath every time she sees the thing."

Half-price was what Morton had paid, and drunk as he was this one time, he would have paid more. He'd turned it on as soon as he got home from the Royalty, and his cat's back had arched, the hair standing up on Christy as she hissed but held her ground. The robot had whirred and crept along, looking adorable if you thought the expression on a painted face was formed exclusively from you being close by.

Morton had played with it for an hour that first night, long enough for him to sober up some and for Christy to bat at it with a paw. Though, finally, in what looked to Morton as cat disgust, Christy abandoned it and him for the spare room, where she stayed under the months-unmade pull-out bed, until the following morning.

By its third night in the apartment, the robot cat joined old magazines and CD cases and pizza boxes as things to step around. Christy seemed triumphant. The cat sat on top of a chair just above the robot, holding her pose for so long he nicknamed her "the gargoyle," calling her that for another three days until the whole miserable sequence faded.

Gerber, he knew from the bartender confirming during his third and last visit to the Royalty, had gone to that bar just the one time two days after the fight. Morton heard he was commuting to Sorensville, five miles of back road driving, to drink. And each night it occurred to Morton that there was a chance, with such a stretch to maneuver, that Gerber would wrap himself and that girl around a tree, but the newspaper never reported it.

* * *

Without the Westberg, and with the Royalty a bad call, Morton started stacking cases of used returnables in his kitchen. He preferred his beer in bottles, but he never got around to putting the empties in his car for a refund trip to the distributor. Staying in gave him more time to ponder questions like, *Where do you meet a woman when you're thirty-five?* Already the ones in their early twenties, like Callie Wertz, seemed like girls, and people like Joe Gerber or better versions of him paired off or surrounded them, competing. He was too old for that dance, and the women who occasionally shopped at Builders Paradise were housewives or single mothers scraping by, heavy with cheap food and exhaustion. The girls he'd known in high school seemed years older than him now. They were on second husbands or second or third men they lived with. They had kids who were nearly grown, hulking sixteen-year-olds who had drivers' licenses and girls of their own. If there were a thirty-year-old attractive woman without commitments, she was as rare as an albino deer, something so striking she would be singled out for fortune or doom.

Question two was always, *What do you have going for yourself?* His answers unfurled in stops and starts like a cheap, tiny flag: Despite his drinking, he'd taken care of himself. His only bar food vice was chicken wings, and he kept them to twice a week. His only impulse food was delivered pizza, food so easy it was more of a habit than a meal. The good news was the rest of the day was power bars and orange juice and a hundred sit-ups before he drove to the Westberg. His gut was thick but firm, not pronounced enough to ruin his confidence, and finally, four weeks into his sentence, Morton showered after work for the first time in a month. "You're short now," he said to himself. "Let's get back in the world."

He drove to Sorensville and walked into each of its three bars to have a beer and evaluate. The first was full of professionals. There was a high school and a high tech business and a newspaper in Sorensville. These people, by their clothes and haircuts, worked at one of those places. But even though they were dressed differently and the jukebox played rock music he didn't recognize, everybody looked under thirty, as if there were a ten o'clock curfew for people his age who were educated.

He played the jukebox in the second, heads turning when his selections—Metallica and AC/DC—came on. "You favor that shit?" one guy hollered from where he was standing at the end of the bar. "That what they like where you come from?" A man beside the music critic had a laugh loud enough to sound like a dare.

Somebody else must play those songs, Morton thought, but it suddenly seemed like that would happen early in the evening, those selections made by a man passing through or by a group headed for the professional bar thinking a pit stop here was a finger-in-the-eye of country and western junkies.

Gloriously, in the third bar the jukebox was a constant. Creed, Kid Rock, Godsmack—the standards he knew from the Westberg. Two pool tables were steady with players. He ordered a second draft, fingered the quarters in his pocket, and then he heard Joe Gerber's voice from halfway down the bar. "You hate making them pussy drinks?" Gerber was asking, but the bartender didn't answer, and Gerber raised his voice as if he needed to be heard in the men's room. "Maybe you stop making that sweet shit, it would thin out the faggots and this place wouldn't suck so much."

Gerber, although he was standing just three stools down, didn't seem to see him, even when he turned with two drafts to walk across the room. Trolling for women, Morton thought, but a minute later, when Creed started up again, he sighed and swiveled just enough to see where Gerber was sitting.

It was a different girl than the one from the Westberg. One more notch to the left of plain. Younger. Definitely underage. Beneath the table, Joe Gerber had his hand under the girl's skirt. She had her legs pressed together, but his hand pushed until her thighs opened just enough for his hand to slip between them. Her eyes fluttered around the room, and Morton knew she was embarrassed, checking for anyone who noticed. Only a man not talking to anyone or not watching television would see this, Morton thought. Only a man alone. Gerber's hand pushed farther and the girl squirmed, took a drink from her beer and scanned the room again, flicking past him and then reversing, coming back and holding his eyes for a moment before she turned sideways from Gerber, his hand slipping out.

Gerber swiveled, lifted his mug, and said, "Cunt," clearly and loudly before he drank. A couple of heads turned as Gerber drank, and the girl blushed, tucking her skirt down.

And then Gerber stood, looked down at her, and said, "Fucking cunt," in the steady, controlled voice of someone calling roll on the first day of school, the words sounding like a first and last name he was making sure he pronounced correctly before he carried the empty mug to a spot at the bar six stools down.

Morton turned toward the television, unable to allow that girl to look his way again. A baseball game from Philadelphia was on, the eleventh inning, but he'd inherited rooting for Baltimore from his father. What happened in the National League was as interesting as a kitchen appliance infomercial.

And when nobody else seemed prepared to mind Joe Gerber's tongue, Morton left half of his beer unfinished and drove the five miles to Westberg so slowly he began to imagine he'd taken the wrong road, and the forest on either side might not open into the eight blocks of houses and businesses that accounted for Westberg's place on the map.

* * *

When he weighed himself on a Builders Paradise bathroom scale the next morning, Morton learned he'd gained ten pounds since the fight. During the next week, he lost five of them just by not drinking after dinner, and by walking five miles or more in the two hours he kept himself outside. With nothing to do one rainy night, he filled three garbage bags and vacuumed the carpets, replaced the CDs in their cases, and slid each one into a slot. He picked up the robot cat, but its batteries were dead, and he placed it on the back of the toilet in the bathroom, the room Christy never entered. By the end of the second week he'd lost three more of the pounds, and when he told Ron and Jake about his housecleaning at work the day his sentence ended, they laughed. "You might as well be married then," Ron said.

"Starting tonight, big fellow, and you can fuck up your place again in style," Jake said. "This is like New Year's Eve in August."

"I'll have my weight back where it belongs if I stay on schedule for a couple more days."

"Walk all the fuck you want then, but just don't you pick a fight. The Westberg's just like a wife. You keep your hands to yourself and she'll be good to you."

"If bars had tits, the Westberg would have a perfect pair," Ron said, and all three of them laughed.

"If it had itself a pussy," Jake said. "I'd never leave."

* * *

"Welcome back, Kotter," the bartender shouted at midnight, and a row of guys, including Ron and Jake, started a chorus, but all they remembered was the "welcome back, welcome back, welcome back."

Morton arched his eyebrows like Gabe Kaplan doing Groucho Marx in an episode he remembered watching in third grade. Nobody seemed to get it, but there was no sign of Gerber, who could have walked in simultaneously, but hadn't, a good enough start. Maybe that place in Sorensville had taken to his idea of serving only shots and beer. "Good to have your fucking ass sitting here again," Ron said, raising his beer in salute.

Morton sucked down his draft in two long gulps and checked the room for assholes, noting Steve Bell and Lon Portzline, who were there, he was suddenly sure, to greet Joe Gerber. They were ordinary jerks, small-time bullies, but he needed to keep a steady head now. Like the way he was around the boss at work at Builders Paradise. There was always shit to take, but if you gave it time, it always rolled off.

While the bartender filled his mug, Morton counted the names on the fight-list behind the bar. It started in 1984 with eight names on the six-week side he didn't recognize. In 1985, the only names were Larry Lebda and Park Mayhew, and when he saw Mayhew's name on the 1987 lifetime list, he knew he'd been talking to Lebda a few weeks back.

The names thinned out fast, especially on the lifetime side. Altogether there were forty-four, including his and Joe Gerber's on the six-week list, but there were just seven on the lifetime side. Banishment was as good a deterrent as the A-Bomb.

Callie walked up and slapped him on the back. "I think I'm pregnant," she said, laughing. "I need to get drunk before I find out for sure and have to stop drinking."

"Six weeks," Kratzer said. "Second time past the time, you know. Twice around don't lie."

"Maybe it was that night," Callie said. "You were such a hero and shit. We didn't get out of the parking lot before Wayne here was inside me."

He glanced at the clock. 12:30, and his sense of triumph was disappearing. When the bartender set a fresh draft in front of him, Kratzer slid six quarters across its path. "We'll name him after you," he said.

"Or her," Callie said, "like Ricki Lake."

"The fat Ricki Lake or the skinny one?" Kratzer said. He looked at Morton as if they shared a secret. "You got to be careful which one you're doing the naming after."

* * *

Halfway through Kratzer's beer, Morton heard Steve Bell shout, "Back in the game," and he didn't have to turn to know Gerber was there.

"Nothing's changed," Gerber said. "I see the same faces right down to teacher come back to watch over homeroom."

The girl from Sorensville was with him, wearing a skirt again, something so odd in the Westberg that Morton guessed it was by request, that Gerber had grown accustomed to having a hand high on her thighs while he drank.

Morton finished Kratzer's beer, and Ron set him up again. "A triple play of Metallica," Jake said, pumping a fist as he came back from the jukebox. "For the prodigal son," he added a beat late, the words sounding like an afterthought.

Morton tensed, figuring this for a straight line for Gerber, but so far, except for naming him "teacher," Gerber hadn't caught his eye or spoken loudly, and just then, as Jake steadied himself on his stool, he recognized what a difference the two of them having a three-hour head start made. The cadence of their speech was out of sync, both of them talking as slowly as stroke victims, and he concentrated on Metallica. Their talk drifted away until he heard Ron say, "Halfway to paradise," in such a clipped tone that he looked and saw Gerber's arm was already up to the elbow under the girl's skirt.

The girl stared at the jukebox like Metallica was in concert there, and it seemed to Morton that Gerber had picked a table against the opposite wall so that his handwork was more visible to anyone seated at the bar. "Oh, fuck me if she's not wearing panties," Jake said, but Morton was already on his feet.

Before he reached Gerber's table, Morton realized his friends would see it as his ridding the Westberg of Joe Gerber, sacrificing himself, his name repeated on the lifer side right above Joe Gerber's. It was such a sensible conclusion, nobody would guess he'd been looking forward to lifting himself off his stool and striding right into Joe Gerber, launching a punch before Gerber got out of his chair.

Morton was glad when Gerber, for a second or two, acted as if he didn't want to fight, maybe keep his name on the temporary side of the banishment list by not taking a swing. He went after Gerber's ribs as he tried to stand, and when Gerber threw his first desperate round house, Morton ducked and drove a knee up into his crotch.

And then he just concentrated on thumping Gerber because this was how he'd be talked about at the Westberg, the man who kicked some fucker's ass twice, a record setter, an hour back and out for life. Morton was saying goodbye. Shouting it so everybody could hear.

SOMEBODY SOMEWHERE ELSE

THE TOURISTS WHO COME year round expecting flames and giant cracks in the earth are always disappointed. The ones who come in summer see how the trees are still green not so far away as in any another town. The ones who come in winter see how grass grows where the soil is warmed from below by the fire. All of them take their photographs where things look worst to show to relatives and friends.

My name is Harold Plezik, retired two years from Penn Modular Homebuilders, and the rest of us who live here, my wife Melinda and fifteen others, they seldom walk out to where the fire has crept. They say there's no curiosity for what's been seen for most of their lives. They act as if they're long past wanting to scold those camera bugs aloud.

The last to leave is what the seventeen of us are called, but that's just out and out wrong, since we're not leaving Centralia, not any of us scattered along Troutwine Street and beyond. Not that the press has shown up for these past five years or so, as if our story has ended or is inching along as slowly as the underground fire that ruined Centralia so long ago that my children, full-grown for years now, were still under my roof.

Everybody knows the story, or they should. Centralia is the town that was burned out from underneath, the seams of coal below us and places nearby smoldering now for going on fifty years. Those newspapers, they'll be back, for sure, when there's half a century of fire, but that's four years off, forever for a reporter. And to tell the truth, we look to be diminishing, trickling away to senior centers or death, nobody here as young as me and Melinda, past sixty now.

And the houses, too. We're on our own inside the last eight of them, the rest long gone. Just the bare spots to be made out where they stood, and the shrubbery and such left to go wild in rows as strange as the telephone poles going nowhere on streets entirely deserted.

A ghost town, some would say, though I think it will never get to be that, what with the government taking down the houses as soon as the owners get committed by their children or die. Somebody would have to rebuild Centralia to make it a ghost town, put up a thousand houses with nothing inside but memories.

Here's one, for instance. There was a time when the *National Enquirer* came to town expecting to see hell right up on the surface. They were disappointed to find just steam and warm earth, but they got the story they wanted by setting a pile of trash on fire to get flames in their pictures and claiming you could fry an egg on the sidewalk as if all of us who used that sidewalk wore some sort of magical insulated boots to retrieve our mail.

That's all you need to hear about that, and frankly, I've had enough of telling people about the history of Centralia. Once upon a time, that sort of talk was for those who'd been taught to unravel things and investigate and pick around papers in libraries and courthouses. These days I want only to talk about the here and now of flesh and blood still standing on the earth that's been left unbroken. The underground fire has moved on, following coal seams, the experts declare, that will last for a century or more.

For example, the man and the girl I came across yesterday.

I'd crossed Route 61 where it's been blocked by a levee of earth for going on twenty years. There's plenty of dead forest out beyond the highway, the trees a dozen shades of near-white from the fire passing beneath them, but there's still green a short hike away, and that's where I was headed, because I have a doctor who's told me to get out of my house or they'll carry me out.

There was a car parked with its tail end right up to that road-block, facing out as if the driver expected to be boxed in by a crowd of sightseers. Not that unusual except the car was parked on the other side of the dirt levee where what was left of the road hasn't had traffic for twenty years. Still, I didn't pay it any mind but to wish whoever owned it not to be a man taking pictures of his wife where I could see, or worse, a teenager drinking beer with his friends and trying to set paper on fire by laying it on the ground.

It was neither, but right off I wished it were one or the other, because there was a man wearing a ball cap and a thin young woman hand in hand ahead and off to my left, the man pushing aside branches as if he were looking for a secluded spot to get laid. What did he think? There was privacy there because the world's moved on? And then I could see that it wasn't a thin woman at all, but a girl of maybe nine or ten, not anybody who belonged where he looked to be leading her. I cut toward them, all three of us in the green part of the woods where undergrowth, in mid-summer, had sprung up thick.

There wasn't even a path to speak of where the man and the girl were walking, though when the man noticed me, he turned and began to double back, and I started to take note of his shadowed face, looking for what the police always call "distinguishing marks." "Hey there," I called from what used to be porch-to-porch distance where Melinda and I still managed to live on Troutwine Street.

"Hi," he said, but he didn't stop, no reason to, perhaps, if all we had in common was being in the same place. He glanced down at the girl and kept his eyes there. She didn't look up, but I thought he tugged just a bit harder on her hand.

For a few seconds I kept my eye on them, and then I followed after, considering on shortening the distance between us. I wished, for once, I carried one of those skinny phones everybody owns now, but I stayed close enough to maybe make me more than curious in that man's mind. And then I thought to speed up to take a look at a license plate at least, but by then they were in the car, and he pulled around the barrier just high enough to keep me from seeing whatever numbers and letters he had on that plate, until he was far enough away to turn them to the fuzz I see at a distance with the glasses years past being the right prescription. The plate was a Pennsylvania one. I could tell that by the colors, but I didn't even know the make or model of the car except to remember it was maroon and small.

I took myself three slow breaths and stood on the shoulder where the cracks from thirty years ago lay as open and dark as old promises. A young couple got out of a blue car parked near the old playground. The girl could have been the child's older sister. Sixteen maybe. Thin. A beauty. The two of them stared at the rusted pipes with no idea, I was sure, of what had been there. I felt as if I'd eaten something turned wrong in the heat. I walked back into the woods where it was green and circled around for an hour as if I were guarding something.

"You see families all the time over that way," Melinda said when I returned and told her about the man and the young girl. "You said he answered when you spoke. He said 'hello' just like anyone would. That makes them sightseers. Their kind have the run of where it's burning."

"This wasn't family business."

"You think a man is evil because he's walking in the woods with a young girl?"

"He wasn't her father. You can tell fathers by the way girls her age walk with them. They look at the man. They lead. This girl was following."

Melinda considered on that. She took her time picturing before she finally said, "Resisting?"

"Reconsidering."

"You can't be sure."

"Sure enough."

"Then report it. Go to the police and tell them you know the man had plans for that girl."

It was good advice, but there was nothing I could do for that girl now but hope.

* * *

For most of his grown life, my father sold insurance to miners. The cheap kind—low payments and lower benefits. The business had dried up with the mines, but he kept his office in Ashland, just down the road where a statue of Whistler's Mother looked over the downtown like something washed up in a great flood. Growing up, I'd asked about that statue, but my father simply said, "It's always been there," and after a while I didn't care whether or not Whistler himself had something to do with Ashland. After all, I didn't live there, and in Centralia, we had the fire to hold my attention.

There's books about how the thing started in a landfill and all the rest that followed, how the powers-that-be argued about responsibility and cost until it was too late. I never read them. What's the point of a book when the story's in your own backyard?

And when the word spread any way it could, the world coming to gawk at a town on fire didn't do a thing to help us, not even when Elsie Turkovich died in her basement a quarter mile from us. She didn't have a carbon monoxide alarm like many of us had acquired by then. My father's company balked at paying. "It's not an accident if someone sleeps downstairs in Centralia," they said. My father stopped selling. He was embarrassed.

After that, it seemed to him, most days, that his life was like that coal seam, that all of whatever was inside him worth a damn just needed air to burn. He'd lived long enough to believe that he'd prefer a few years or even months of flame to the eternal smoldering where there was so little oxygen any other fire would just go out.

He must have felt that way right up to his death, unable, near the end, to even get from one room to another without the humiliating walker. Maybe it was worse for him knowing the fire hadn't changed anything, because he'd been forty years old when it started, and he'd known for years what he was about.

Though he never claimed he hadn't had a fair chance, the excuse, he told me, of the poor in spirit, who put too much stock in the Beatitudes. He kept his mouth shut forever against the shame of admitting he had thoughts in that direction. And when he died, he made sure he was in the hospital so people with authority could testify he'd had a natural death.

* * *

Here's something to consider: A while back our mayor was on television. *The Daily Show*. They sent out this fake reporter whose job it was to make a fool of him.

A mayor for twenty people in a burning town. Hilarious. The audience laughed. I wanted to kill that fake. "Maybe when he gets cancer someone will make fun of his wearing a hat to cover his bald head," I said.

Melinda frowned just the small bit she does for a piece of fruit gone quickly soft on the kitchen counter before she said, "Hush, it's just a show."

"He was on our street," I said. "On Troutwine. In Lamar's house for a big joke. I hope it's the kind that disfigures him."

* * *

I made myself wait two days before I went out to where I'd seen the man and girl. Nobody had gone missing in the local paper, but for all I knew he'd driven here from a hundred miles away like somebody smart about doing evil would do.

I wasn't fifty feet from the road before I caught sight of my first tourists. Three of them. A woman my age. Two much younger. "We came to see the fire," the older woman said. "We didn't know anybody lived here."

She let me know she was the mother of the female half of the married couple already at a distance from where we were standing. Her daughter and son-in-law were over by the edge of where the trees were still green, and the man, who looked to be thirty or thereabouts, had his feet set wide apart as if he were trying to straddle a border. "You live around here?" she said, and I nodded, but she didn't ask me to pinpoint. "All this is burning?" she asked instead, swinging her head left to right in a way that included the still healthy forest.

"Where the trees are white," I said.

"Big as that?" She gestured toward her daughter. "You hear that? The fire is all over out here."

I turned away. Let her go home, wherever that was, thinking places the fire had passed were still on fire, as if coal could regenerate itself. I made a point to cross into the shade before I reached the couple, but they were already headed toward a spot where coal was exposed and steaming. I walked a hundred yards until it felt as if I couldn't be seen by them. There was a fallen tree that made for a bench. When I sat down the woods seemed as private as a bathroom with the door locked.

For an hour I listened.

* * *

My son Daniel was in the living room when I came in the door. "You have that look," he said at once. "What's up?"

"I had to talk to tourists."

"If you go out there, that's what you'll see, Dad. That's who's in the woods—tourists."

"You sound like your mother, but neither of you go out there anymore. There's not so many nearby now. It was more fun for them when the fire was closer to town."

Daniel had moved when the government was offering money for our houses, when there was a rash of the red Xs that they spray painted on the front to let the bulldozers know which ones were ready to raze. It was like Passover in reverse. The angel of death came for those houses in a bulldozer.

"Mom told me you saw the boogie man a few days ago."

I glanced toward the kitchen where Melinda was fussing with making lemonade. "A particular kind."

Whatever was in my face turned him serious. "Ok," he said. "I'll grant you it's possible."

"Possible enough to keep me fretting I didn't take after him."

"What makes you the Good Samaritan all of a sudden?" Daniel said, and I thought of that child getting back into the maroon car, whether she knew by then that there couldn't be any puppies or kittens or whatever that man had promised to show her in a place like Centralia where children hadn't lived since before she was born.

"It's not all of a sudden. Somebody doesn't get that many chances to come across those that need help."

"Everybody needs help, Dad. If you want to be part-time Jesus, just admit it."

"You can't expect others to do what needs to be done."

"That's just the government."

Melinda stepped in between us with the lemonade in tall glasses half filled with ice. If we didn't finish our drinks within minutes, they would turn to dishwater with the melting. "The police is government," I said, not letting her barge in between us with words.

"They're close by. That makes a difference."

"We don't own our house bought and paid for all these years," I said. "That's government."

"They don't put you out."

Melinda said, "Now the both of you drink your drinks. There's more where they came from. This is visit time, not a debate."

Daniel took a sip, and I could tell he'd grown unused to lemonade being on the sour side. "You could see the future when I was a kid, Dad. Eminent domain is just the end of it coming. There's nothing to be done anymore except to let it run its course."

"All the more reason to pay attention to what's terrible."

"There's nothing to do about that either, Dad. Not now anyway."

"You know what I wish," I said, staring at Melinda as I spoke, "I wish I was the sort of man who could kill such assholes as that fellow in the woods, do some subtraction from the evil side of things."

"Stop it, Dad," Daniel said, but Melinda was the one staring at me now.

"You imagine yourself becoming the eye-for-an-eye man, Harold?" she said. "You keep in mind he hasn't killed anyone we know of."

"Yes, he has."

"God doesn't see it that way."

"God has it wrong then."

"You best be keeping that talk to yourself."

"I have worse I'm thinking."

* * *

I had my palm read once by Mrs. Yanoviak, who lived across the street until she died when I was near forty, about the time Daniel moved and the houses were torn down as soon as they were unoccupied. Within weeks. Like filling in a grave before the mourners are out of sight.

Mrs. Yanoviak held my hand in hers and concentrated as if there might be a difference between the lines on my palm and the ones on every other human hand. I was twenty-two at the time, three years under my belt with making modular homes and married to Melinda with Clarice on the way. Old lady Yanoviak, she stared and said, "You need to have yourself checked now that the baby's coming."

She went on for a few minutes, but all I was listening for was the prophecy of my lifeline, whether it was long enough to keep worry away for the next fifty years. "You'll live a good long time," she said. "It's plain as day."

"Methuselah," I said.

"Don't you be thinking that way," she said. "God shortened us for a reason back then. He'd learned that seventy years was enough for people to prove what was in their hearts."

When I brought up Mrs. Yanoviak after Daniel left, Melinda and I were standing on the front porch. She shrugged. "You and me lived here long enough to lose our illusions," she said. "If that's a good thing, then we're full of goodness."

I sucked one of the lemonade's nearly melted ice cubes into my mouth and held it there until it disappeared. Years ago, after Clarice and Daniel had grown and gone, I'd learned that having little was what could keep people together. Without the kids in the house, we'd been subtracted down to ourselves and the idea that it was important to stay no matter what.

It hadn't taken long to lose some of both of those things. The town nearly emptied. We were fools now, people the government didn't bother asking to pay. And nearing, then passing fifty, Melinda and I grew leery of each other's bodies, seeing the age in ourselves reflected so harshly we stopped wanting to touch.

"We live where we know who we are," I said at last, sounding so awful to myself I expected Melinda to hiss.

She took my lemonade glass from my hand, the last three ice cube slivers drifting in the puddle at the bottom. "You look up and down this street and tell me who we are, Harold."

Three vacant lots separated us from the two other houses on our side of the street. On the other side were two houses four lots apart. "The Kelmans and the Mischiks have it OK being side by side," I tried. "I expect that makes a difference, seeing a face at a window from time to time instead of all this flat."

"Old man Mischik is all alone in that house of his, and he's ready to croak," she said. "The Kelmans will be like us inside of a year."

I have to say I flinched at the word *croak*. It sounded as if Melinda had said, "Fuck off," like dying was the sort of dismissal you might give a possum or some other scavenger you know you need but don't want to see. "We're going extinct," I said, "and what's worse, we know it. We're not like dodos or passenger pigeons or whatever else is dead and gone."

"I bet they knew," she said. "Leastways the last ones. They must have looked around and seen. They must have wondered where everybody had gone off to."

"Such things don't wonder."

"Don't you count on that," she said. "Everything with a beating heart knows when aloneness has come to stay."

* * *

These girls came out here once, six of them from a university that makes them volunteer. S.A.V.E. they called themselves, the E for environment, and they were dressed to clean up after the tourists for us as if they were going to work at the mall.

Three more followed. Older ones. Professors maybe, in hiking boots at least, and the lot of them put dirt into dozens of test tubes out among where all of the trees are gray and white. Those three were polite about taking what they wanted from us. Studying bacteria, they said, when I approached them, but they didn't explain how that could matter to somebody, and they didn't ask me one word about my living there.

* * *

Melinda asked to come along when I went for another walk the next day. "I haven't been in a while," she said.

We crossed where St. Ignatius used to stand, the building long gone, but its cemetery and the two others nearby still there, all three resting places untouched by the fire when it passed by. Melinda made me walk straight through it as if she believed that path would somehow settle me. Even the tombstones farthest to the edge, ones worn down a bit by the acid rain, were still in place. "Everybody's at peace here, Harold, no matter the fire. You know there's God when you see something like this," she said. "The living have to take care of themselves, but he's looking out for the dead."

I examined the stones by the fence, all of the dead as old as the two of us or older. "They all died before the fire," Melinda said. "It didn't touch them, not any way at all."

We walked out to a cluster of sinkholes where the smell of sulfur made us watch each step. What looked to be a family was out ahead of us. A child ran across a patch of exposed, steaming coal. A boy, something to be glad for. "You want to head over to the living woods?" Melinda said. "Show me where your troubles began?"

I watched that boy run for a moment. He waved at his parents as if he were on a ride at Disney World. "The outsiders used to be afraid of us," I said. "They'd think that we could go crazy with our anger, hurt one of them or worse because bum luck frees you to do most anything."

"That's so much foolishness, Harold," she said. "You don't know the minds of others."

The boy's father knelt and placed his hand on the earth, but his wife kept walking. "Nowadays they know better," I said. "If we were going to do harm to them, that time has passed. Now they know we could only hurt each other and probably not even that."

"Like normal folks," she said, and I nodded.

"Like the beaten."

"You can't talk like that," she said. "Not with how we're here and not leaving ever except by carrying."

I touched one of the large stones I'd seen tourists use as chairs. It was warm, but not hot, and I slumped down and went silent for a minute, long enough for her to say, "Harold? Where'd you go off to?"

"I'm right here."

She stood behind me and placed her hands on my shoulders, kneading them softly until I raised my head and looked at her placid face. "I thought maybe you took me wrong there when I was meaning to be cheerful," she said. When I shook my head, she leaned down and kissed my cheek.

"We're the Centralians, Harold," Melinda whispered into my ear. "We're from some place."

* * *

The paper comes late half of the time, so we were finished with our toast and cereal the next morning when I heard the deliveryman's car pause at the box. Because Melinda was still in her nightgown, I went out, so I was the first one, coming back through the kitchen door, to see the lead story. How there'd been a body found in the woods ten miles from here, out past Ashland. A girl, the police were saying, who looked to be between eight and ten.

I sat for a minute, holding the paper face down, my stomach working like I had the flu coming on, and then I pushed up from the table and threw up in the sink.

"Harold," Melinda said. "Harold?" and I turned the tap to wash my breakfast away, seeing that girl's face so plain I might as well have her photograph on the mantle.

Melinda turned the paper over. "It can't be the same girl," she said. "They don't say anything about what state they found her in."

"You mean decomposed?" I said. "Like he took her those ten miles before he felt the world was empty enough to do what he wanted?"

"Just hold on with your thinking," she said, up and going into the living room to turn on the television. "They've had half a day to find out. You sit here and watch with me so I can keep my eye on you."

It took twenty minutes of talk about a new movie, a diet plan, and another new gadget to plug in your ears before the Wilkes-Barre area headlines came on with a picture of a girl named Muriel Haskins from Pottsville, another ten miles beyond where they found her. Melinda took my hand in hers and squeezed. I could hear how she was holding her breath, but I knew at once that it wasn't the girl I'd seen that day.

I waited until Muriel's picture was replaced by a photograph of a badly damaged car, before I said, "It's not her."

"One small blessing," Melinda said.

"Not hardly. He just bided his time until another one let herself be used."

"You don't know for sure it's the same man. It's not likely he'd let himself do such a thing so close by after you saw him."

"Then there's two of the devil."

Melinda turned the television to mute as if she'd heard a car in the driveway and was listening for a knock. "You saved one, Harold."

"An accident."

"That's how most saving gets done."

I dressed and drove to Ashland, and when I said I had information related, maybe, to the killing, I saw expressions change to something other than welcoming, just before one of the policemen asked me to take a seat beside his desk.

"What sort of information?" he said. I lowered my voice, as if I had a secret to keep from the others.

He took my name and all that sort of thing after I finished narrowing his suspects down to maybe half of the owners of small maroon cars in Pennsylvania. "You find that girl I saw," I said, "and she'll know something more."

"That's possible," he said.

"She must live around here."

"That's possible as well."

"Around here," I said. "'Around here,' like that meant something. Goddamn, but I must sound like some old idiot spouting off."

"Anger is a gift sometimes," the policeman said.

Anger is a gift. I'd read that somewhere growing up and then, years later, had heard somebody spouting that very line on a CD Daniel played at deaf-inducing volume, repeating the phrase as if he'd just thought it up.

"Yes, it is," I said, believing it now, and I wished for anger rather than the soul-killing surrender that waited for me each morning like a hangover. There were more days than not when the self-indulgence of sorrow absorbed as many hours as a full-time job.

I rose from my chair, but the policeman stayed seated. "Well," I said. "I'm sorry I don't have more for you."

"You can only tell me what you know. You're not required to know more than that."

And then it came to me that the man in the ball cap had spoken. "He said 'hi,'" I blurted. "The man in the woods. He spoke to me."

The policeman leaned forward a bit, both elbows on his desk. "What did he sound like?"

I sat and thought, listening to that memory for nearly a minute. "Like anyone," I said.

The policeman nodded as if that were exactly how every suspect sounded. "That fire over your way creeps along at its own good time," he said.

"Slower these days, it seems, or because it's off to make somebody else's misery."

"Like most folks do," he said, and his lips opened slightly, as if a smile might work its way to the surface. When it didn't, his face froze into acknowledgement. "It makes you wonder sometimes. There's coal all around here. For miles in every direction."

* * *

"Daniel called," Melinda said before I even recounted my trip. "He's heard the news."

"When it's on the television, he listens."

She handed me the phone. "Just hold this a minute," she said. "You need to think twice before you call him."

I held the phone as if it were a glass of lemonade. "It seems like we don't know what's happening to us except when the heart of it's passed us by," I said. "We only know what's dead and gone."

"Let's hope not."

"For sure, we can always do that."

"It's some relief."

I imagined that girl in the woods taking my hand as soon as I offered it, and I wasn't glad for that because it would be better if she cried to show me she'd learned something. "You ever want to be somebody else?" I said.

"Like who?"

"Somebody somewhere else."

"There's no point to that sort of wishing. It's like hoping you'll sprout wings."

"There's plenty wasting themselves then," I said, and I pressed *memory* and 1 for Daniel's number. Clarice, if I decided to call her in Colorado so far away, was 2. If Melinda had programmed numbers up to 9, I didn't know who they'd be for.

* * *

Last fall a girl drove up from that university of the volunteers. I recognized her parking sticker when she pulled into Lamar's driveway. More mayor jokes, I thought, but when she left, Lamar came over to tell me how she'd interviewed him the right way. He was beaming as if he'd met his granddaughter full-grown after twenty years. "For a magazine they do down there," he said. "Pictures and all."

I have a copy of that magazine on a table beside the couch. Lamar gave it to me a month back, thick and glossy like you wouldn't expect from a college. Our house is in one of the pictures, and so are the sinkholes out by the woods where that ball cap man was taking that girl.

* * *

It's been a month now and no more news. Melinda claims a goodness in that, but I sit with this daydream of finding that man and taking him back to where the fire burns hottest under the soil. "I want you to dig yourself a hole where the fire is," I say every time.

There's always a rifle in my hand, and the man's hands shake so much I am almost happy. "You can't just dig like this where the fire sits," the man says. "You don't know how close it is."

"Then there's no telling how far you have to go before we find out."

When I told Melinda that way of my thinking, she turned afraid for my soul. Her very words.

"It's just thinking," I told her. "Remember that boy from down the street who the papers and magazines said fell through the earth and almost went into the fire? It was an old sewer put in years ago that was covered over with planks instead of being capped. They rotted out is all. They had him going halfway to hell, a good story, that one, like the ones in the Bible where everything happens for a lesson. But if you live through it, you know the extent of the lies and such, the stories people tell to comfort themselves."